*"Have you completely lost your mind?"* Nikki yelled as Josh slammed on the brakes and the car lurched to a halt.

"It's you I don't know anymore," he said softly, his eyes glittering with fury.

Her heart jumped into her throat. She tried to move away to the safety of her side of the car, but he was having none of it. His hands tightened on her arms. "It's game time, Nikki, and the game is Twenty Questions. My questions. Your answers."

A tremor coursed down her spine, and she squirmed, testing the strength of his grip and finding it unbreakable. "You're scaring me, Josh," she said, confessing her fear in hopes it would bring him to his senses.

"Then we're even. You've scared me plenty in the last couple of hours, and I don't take that from anybody."

His arrogance sparked her anger back to life. "Let go of me, Josh. Ask whatever you want, but let go of me."

"Lady," he whispered between his teeth, "I'm not even close to letting you go." Before she could protest, he bent his head and took her mouth in a fierce kiss. She gasped and struggled, but she was helpless to break free. Suddenly he stopped, his mouth still on hers, and with a soft moan he traced her lips with his tongue. The gentle touch and aching sound went through her like heated honey, melting every ounce of sense she had. . . .

## WHAT ARE *LOVESWEPT* ROMANCES?

They are stories of true romance and touching emotion. We believe those two very important ingredients are constants in our highly sensual and very believable stories in the *LOVESWEPT* line. Our goal is to give you, the reader, stories of consistently high quality that may sometimes make you laugh, sometimes make you cry, but are always fresh and creative and contain many delightful surprises within their pages.

Most romance fans read an enormous number of books. Those they truly love, they keep. Others may be traded with friends and soon forgotten. We hope that each *LOVESWEPT* romance will be a treasure—a "keeper." We will always try to publish

*LOVE STORIES YOU'LL NEVER FORGET*
*BY AUTHORS YOU'LL ALWAYS REMEMBER*

The Editors

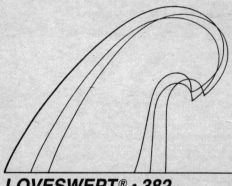

LOVESWEPT® • 382

# Glenna McReynolds
# Dateline: Kydd
# and Rios

BANTAM BOOKS
NEW YORK • TORONTO • LONDON • SYDNEY • AUCKLAND

To Sue, Steve, Mike,
and Kristen with love.

DATELINE: KYDD AND RIOS

*A Bantam Book / February 1990*

*LOVESWEPT® and the wave device are registered
trademarks of Bantam Books, a division of
Bantam Doubleday Dell Publishing Group, Inc.
Registered in U.S. Patent
and Trademark Office and elsewhere.*

*If you would be interested in receiving protective vinyl
covers for your Loveswept books, please write to this address
for information:*

*Loveswept
Bantam Books
P.O. Box 985
Hicksville, NY 11802*

ISBN 0-553-22027-6

*Published simultaneously in the United States and Canada*

---

*Bantam Books are published by Bantam Books, a division
of Bantam Doubleday Dell Publishing Group, Inc. Its trademark, consisting of the words "Bantam Books" and the
portrayal of a rooster, is Registered in U.S. Patent and
Trademark Office and in other countries. Marca Registrada.
Bantam Books, 666 Fifth Avenue, New York, New York 10103.*

---

PRINTED IN THE UNITED STATES OF AMERICA

O    0 9 8 7 6 5 4 3 2 1

# One

Nikki Kydd crawled up the hill, snaking through the rotting vegetation on the forest floor, her knees and elbows working in tandem, keeping low to the ground. At the top of the rise she stopped next to a man dressed in similar olive drab camouflage and pushed her sweat-dampened hair back off her face.

"How does it look? Damn." She slapped at a mosquito biting her neck.

"Bad," he grunted, scanning the horizon with a pair of binoculars.

Nikki grinned, the flash of a mischievous expression showing through the grime streaking her face. "What in the hell did you do to them, Josh?"

"Nothing you wouldn't have done if you'd thought of it first." Josh Rios pushed himself up higher by straightening one arm. The binoculars never budged from his face. "They've got a grenade launcher."

She muttered a curse, and without a second thought she grabbed the binoculars and held them to her eyes. Hanging by the strap around Josh's neck, the binoculars caused his skull to thud against hers.

"Dammit, Nikki. If you were going to konk me, I wish you'd done it before we left Costa Rica."

"Then you would have missed all the fun."

"Some fun." He slipped the strap over his head and rolled over onto his back. Sweat and muck had mingled to form a mask of mud on his forehead and cheeks. He started to wipe at it with his arm, then decided otherwise. Anything was better than being eaten alive by the swarm of black flies buzzing around them.

Relaxing for a moment, he stared up at the canopy of trees poking at the sky. Their thick foliage blocked out all but a few faint gleams of sunlight. He prayed none of the trees would topple over, for experience had taught him they were alarmingly unstable. More than once when bivouacked for the night, he'd heard one of the lofty giants let go of the earth and come crashing down, crushing everything in its path. That he was concerned about such an occurrence bothered him more than the possibility.

He was definitely getting too old to bushwhack these godforsaken Central American rain forests. Well, actually, he wasn't getting too old, but Nikki was. In the year since he'd found her on the streets of San Simeon, they'd been in and out of more scrapes than in all his previous twenty-four years. The girl had a way of finding trouble. She also had a way of finding a story.

"Josh," she hissed. "Get your camera, the telephoto lens. We've got one."

He reacted immediately to her command, forgetting about his weariness in the rush of excitement. All they needed was one good shot; then they could get the hell out of there.

The thought brought him up short again, his hand pausing on his Nikon, his brow furrowing. Damn, he *was* getting old.

"Hurry," Nikki whispered. "They're moving out of the clearing. He's the one in back. Typically." She snorted the last word in disgust.

Josh screwed in the heavy lens—Big Bertha, he called it—and automatically checked the other settings on the Nikon. Thirty seconds later, he had the camera poised and the lens racked out.

"He's American," Josh murmured, "but . . . Ah, I see it." He smiled, focusing on the tiny flash of captain's bars on the man's lapel. "For a military adviser, he's awfully far from base."

"Yeah. I wonder what he's advising them on. How to track nosy reporters through the rain forest?"

"I'm not going to argue politics with you," Josh said, letting his motor drive eat up a roll of film as he scanned the group of men, trying to fit the captain and a recognizable chunk of landscape into the same frame. He and Nikki disagreed on almost everything except how far they'd go to get a story. It made for a stormy relationship sometimes. "Okay, I've got it. Let's go."

He turned toward her, but she was already ten steps ahead of him, slinging her pack over her shoulder and disappearing into the thick undergrowth at the bottom of the hill.

Josh watched her, and found himself thinking all the strange thoughts that had been plaguing him for the last two months, maybe longer if he dared to admit it. Nikki had great breasts, and the way her hips curved into her waist was getting damn hard to ignore. The skinny girl he'd picked up as a stringer and interpreter was becoming a woman before his very eyes. He couldn't shut off his awareness of her, and he didn't know what to do about it. But one thing was clear—they couldn't go on this way, running from one crisis to another, raising hell in every two-bit town in Central America, scooping the other reporters at every opportunity, and griping and complaining when they didn't.

Tonight, Josh, he told himself. Tonight he'd tell her she was going back to the States. He hoped he was up to the fight.

The instant the thought crossed his mind, he knew he wasn't. He was tired of fighting with her, and lately they seemed to do little else. Every conversation they had turned into an argument, and he knew why. Fighting was the only safe avenue for releasing his frustration. When he looked at her, or when she stood too close, he wanted to touch her . . . and touch her again. He wanted to run his thumb along her usually too smart mouth until her lips softened with desire. He wanted to gaze into her sea green eyes until she saw him as a man, until her golden lashes drifted down and she raised her mouth to his. Then he'd kiss her, long and sweet. He would wrap his arms around her waist and pull her close, feeling her breasts press soft and full against his chest; and he'd kiss her some more, sliding his tongue into her mouth and—

"Damn," he muttered, forcing himself back away from the waking fantasy. He'd never make it through the night if he allowed his emotions free rein. Hell, they wouldn't even make it back to the hotel. A part of him insisted on believing that if he made the first move, she would respond. If he kissed her, she'd kiss him back. Of course, the rest of him said he was nuts, the parts of him concerned with survival, with common sense, with continuing to be a free agent.

As he sat there in the dirt arguing with himself and breaking down the camera, a low bank of gray clouds rolled in over the trees, stealing the dim light from the sky. He cursed again and began jamming his gear into his pack, berating himself for being a fool. He'd lost all sense of perspective in his life. Nikki was filling his mind, making him do dumb things like getting caught in the rain. She was probably halfway to the jeep, and he was still screwing around on the hill.

Nikki dashed the last few yards to the jeep, clutching her pack in her arms to keep it dry. Once inside, she slicked her hair away from her face and grabbed a towel out of the back. The thick white terry cloth felt heavenly on her face. It should, she thought. They'd absconded with it out of the best hotel in San Simeon, the Paloma Grand Hotel. Of course, at her insistence, they'd left a neat stack of coins on the bathroom counter. But as she rubbed the luxurious cloth over her face, she wondered if they'd left enough.

The other door was wrenched open, and she heard Josh swearing under his breath as he sloshed into the driver's seat.

"What took you so long?" she mumbled from beneath the towel.

When he didn't reply, she peaked over one heavily embroidered edge of terry cloth. He was sprawled over the steering wheel, his clothes steaming, his head hidden between his arms. Water streamed down the ebony strands of his hair and plastered his shirt to his body, revealing every muscle-hardened curve of his shoulders and biceps. Unbidden, her gaze traced the length of his arms to his large, rough hands, then dropped to his waist, and farther to where his leg rested against the stick shift, only a few inches from hers. A soft explosion of heat burst deep inside her body and trapped her breath in her throat. Jumbled, chaotic images flashed through her mind—of Josh sweeping her into his arms, of his mouth close to her ear, whispering in the dark, of her hand so small and white resting on his tightly corded thigh, her fingers slowly and gently stroking his satiny brown skin.

"Let's get going," she blurted out. "Before the road turns into a swamp. I'd rather spend the night at the hotel than stuck out here."

"Good idea," he mumbled, wiping his face on his sleeve and glancing over his arm. "I could use a cold shower."

His eyes were a dusky blue in the shadows, like a midsummer twilight. They met hers across the vapor-filled interior, and for a moment she forgot not to stare. He was so beautiful, his face, dark and arrogant, chiseled out of a young girl's dreams. A streak of mud slashed down his cheek, concealing the lower half of the scar that traced his hairline. The result of an ill-spent youth on the Texas side of the Rio Grande, he'd told her once with a wry grin. During the past year, she'd imagined and then confronted him with a dozen different scenarios of that ill-spent youth. She'd come up with hair-raising exploits in back-alley street fights and illegal border crossings in the dead of night. He'd never confirmed any of them, but he hadn't denied them either.

Now she wondered anew about the person who had cut him, and she wondered what it would be like to touch that thin white line with her fingertip, to caress his face and take the old hurt away. The heat in her body slowly rose to her face, and she knew she'd looked too long.

"Right. I could use a shower, too," she said quickly. But deep down inside she doubted if the Casa del Flores had enough cold water to cool her down.

True to the hotel's name, spidery boughs of bougainvillea interspersed with cascades of clematis swept around three sides of the Casa del Flores's courtyard. Graceful palm trees swayed and dipped in the evening breeze, the rustling of their fronds lost in the sounds of the dining area. Tomorrow the whole place might go up in flames, but tonight the Casa del Flores was a haven of peace.

Nikki sat hunched over her table, jotting notes by candlelight. Three empty beer bottles flanked a plate of half-eaten beans, rice, and tortillas. She'd picked all the chicken out. If Josh didn't sell a story pretty soon, there wouldn't be any chicken next time. She really had to get on him about it. The figures she quickly added up proved her point. They were running on empty.

Boom or bust, she thought with a disgruntled sigh. Even looking at her notebook, she didn't know where all their money went. There were too many miscellaneous entries—all of them in Josh's handwriting. "Misc." seemed to be his only expenditure.

She flipped to the back pages where they kept their private accounts. Typically, Josh's debits were all labeled "Misc.," the last one nearly three hundred dollars. What in the miscellaneous hell had he done with three hundred dollars? she wondered, wrinkling her brow.

She had very few debits on her private page, just a sure and growing line of credits tucked away in a

Boulder, Colorado, bank. But there weren't enough of them. She needed more money, lots more money. A year of risking her tail in the hottest spots in Latin America hadn't given her the price of one person's freedom.

Unwanted, that knowledge forced its way to the front of her mind, constricting her heart with sadness. Her mouth softened in pain, and suddenly she wished Josh would hurry up and come down to dinner. She didn't like to be left alone with her thoughts, not when they turned to her mother.

A story, Nikki, she told herself. Think of a story, a blockbusting, fortune-making story. They needed a story like the one they'd broken the day she'd gone looking for protection. The day she'd found Joshua Rios. . . .

# *Two*

"General Travinas, the former secretary of defense, and his armed forces stormed the Palacio de Simeon this morning at dawn, taking control of the government. All of the remaining cabinet members—Mendez, Cavazos, and Estrada—were taken hostage. President Aragon is believed to have left the country."

As the radio signal buzzed and cracked its message of anarchy, Nikki shoved a pair of pants, a shirt, a comb, and her toothbrush into a ragged satchel. She'd waited too long. She'd trusted all the wrong people. Her heart beat fast beneath the dirty blouse she'd thrown on. She had to move quickly and find help for herself. It was too late to help her mother now. Until the fires of revolt burned themselves out, no one would risk releasing any political prisoners, and certainly not Helen Kydd Cavazos.

She needed to find an American, and every American left in San Simeon would be on the steps of the palacio, trying to get a story for a newspaper, magazine, or television station. Only the reporters remained in the small country racked by rebellion.

Everyone with any sense had left weeks ago, except Nikki.

Looking around the shabby one-room apartment, she now realized her mistake. Aragon had set them all up, all of his loyal followers, especially Victor Cavazos. He'd sold them down the river. Nikki knew the how, the when, and the why, but she was the only one outside of a prison who did. Aragon had underestimated her if he thought she wouldn't use her knowledge. Or maybe he had dismissed her as a flighty teenager, the mere daughter of the woman he'd never trusted, the wife of his minister of economic development. Or maybe he thought she didn't know the language and politics of his country well enough to understand what she'd seen and heard during palace functions. He was wrong on all counts.

Nikki had liked Victor, her mother's new husband, but the dashing, debonair Latin had proved to be incredibly ineffective in dealing with Aragon. Helen had been under house arrest for a week before the president had thrown her in prison. Victor should have whisked her out of the country long before then.

"Damn Victor," Nikki said under her breath. "Damn his cowardly hide." Now it was up to her to get her mother out of prison, a tricky business, and all she had to exchange for protection was information. Most of the war correspondents she'd met would sell their own grandmothers for a story. She needed somebody more idealistic than that. She needed someone who *looked* as if he knew what he was doing, without knowing exactly what he was doing. Someone who knew exactly what he was doing wouldn't need her for long. He'd take her information and run, either leaving her behind or trying to ship her back home.

And she wasn't leaving without her mother.

Nikki slipped the satchel strap over her shoulder and tried not to think about how dirty she felt. When the chaos had started, the waterworks had been the first casualty. Travinas and Aragon were probably bathing in champagne in the palace, she thought, laughing at the great joke of a coup d'état they'd pulled off. She'd see how hard they laughed when she exposed their corrupt deal to the world. Aragon would be branded for the traitor he was, and—she hoped and prayed—the world would demand the release of the woman he'd unjustly imprisoned.

Without bothering to close the door behind her, Nikki walked out of the room and down the steps to the street. Fifteen minutes of hard walking brought her to the Palacio de Simeon. As she'd expected, the place was swarming with media people. They filled the street leading up to the palace entrance, and spilled into the mob of San Simeonites crowding the parkway. The best of them were jostling for position on the broad granite steps of the connecting government building.

Light from the dying sun gilded the avenue of palms and turned the marble columns fronting the palace into shafts of mauve and pink. The roof of every car was filled to capacity with men and boys whose families and livelihood now depended upon the whims of General Travinas.

Nikki's gaze skipped over the native countrymen and went directly to the men on the steps. From personal experience she eliminated more than half of the reporters, doubting the depth of their gratitude for the story she could give them. A few of the men looked too green, too lost in the commotion. Others looked too drugged and boozed out. The longer she looked, the more unsure she became. Maybe she hadn't thought this thing through well enough. Maybe she should opt for a ticket out of the country and try to garner support from the safety of the United States. Maybe she should . . . *Maybe . . . maybe . . .*

The sudden doubts sent a slowly curling wave of nausea down to her empty stomach. She gritted her teeth and tightened her hand around the satchel strap, her knuckles white with strain. A tickling stream of sweat rolled down her face. Another matted her lashes, and she wiped at it with the back of her dirty hand. She couldn't leave, would never, ever leave, she silently vowed, reaching deep inside herself for the courage she needed. What chance would her mother have if she abandoned her? For all of her doubts, the answer came quick and sure—none. Then she saw him.

Coal black hair gave him a Latino look, but his clothes had "Made in the U.S.A." stamped all over them. He was tall and broad-shouldered, and his eyes were light. He was too young to be burned out, and the way he was fighting his way to the front of the crowd told her plenty about his drive. He was perfect—or rather, as good as she was going to get.

With a barrage of Spanish insults and a few well-placed elbow jabs, she made her own way up the government-building steps to his side.

"Hey, señor. *Habla español?*"

"No, I—" Josh stopped short, his jaw slackening in disbelief as he stared down at the girl tugging on his sleeve. Dressed in rags, she was dirty, and absolutely beautiful. A short crop of white blond hair, barely a shade darker than her pale skin, surrounded a face of purely feminine delicacy. Sea green eyes framed by golden lashes stared back at him, narrowed to an unsettling degree of scrutiny and flashing with impatience. "No, I don't," he finished in confusion.

Perfect, Nikki thought with an inward sigh of relief. "Then you need me. It just so happens I'm available right now—Hey, watch it, gringo!" she snapped at a reporter trying to shove his way past her. When the man didn't retreat, she elbowed him in the side and leveled him with a stream of cussing that left no doubt in Josh's mind about her command of the Spanish language. "A hundred dollars a day"—she looked back up at him—"but I'm negotiable."

"I don't have a hundred dollars a day." Her outlandish request brought a grin to his face.

Had Nikki been of a mind, his smile might have struck a responsive chord somewhere in her emotions. He'd certainly graduated from the tall, dark, and handsome school of good looks. But she had serious business to conduct.

"Don't worry. As I said, I'm negotiable. We can work something out later. Right this minute, there's a story happening, but you're in the wrong place for it."

Josh glanced around him at the crush of reporters and photographers, each and every one of them waiting for a statement from the new president. "All of these guys can't be wrong," he said with another grin.

Her eyes held his for a piercing second. "All of these *guys*," she said coolly, "are going to get half a story, the one the government dishes out like pabulum. If you don't have the guts to find out the other half, then I'm talking to the wrong man."

Her words challenged him on every level: his intelligence, his credibility, his ambition, and his manhood. Coming from a slip of a girl, they angered him. Backed up by those implacable green eyes, they dared him. She was serious, damn serious, and despite her non-native looks, he found himself believing in her.

"Where?" he asked, praying his instincts were right. He'd spent his last dime getting south to the action, and if he wanted to eat for the next week, he had to make the trip pay off quick. For a free-lancer, that meant coming up with something the other guys didn't get. For a skilled photographer who was still a novice reporter, that meant finding someone who could help him. This girl might be the someone.

"Follow me," she said, already moving away from him.

Josh hesitated for a second, but only a second. Whatever was going to go down, it was going to do so pretty damn quick. This was not the time for indecision.

Fighting his way out of the crowd, he kept his eyes trained on her hair, the brightest spot of life in the pushing and shoving mass of humanity. She seemed to have an inborn skill for finding every opening, and only his longer stride enabled him to catch her at the bottom of the steps.

"Where are we going?" he asked, running to keep up with her.

"Around back."

"Why?" While they jogged along, he checked both of his cameras for readiness.

"Travinas will enter through that door." She gestured at a small portico on the side of the palace and kept running.

"So why don't we stop?"

"Because while he's going in, I think some other people are going to be coming out the back. And that's the story we want."

"You think?" Josh grabbed her arm and jerked her to a stop.

"Yes!" She shook herself free and glared at him. "I think! Which is something you better start doing!"

Dammit, he thought, feeling like a fool. He'd given up a hard-won spot on the stairs and followed some green-eyed witch to the deserted back of the building where she *thought* there might be a story. Muttering in disgust, he turned toward the front entrance.

"Look, mister." The edge in her voice cut right through him and stopped him in his tracks. "I'm giving you the chance of a lifetime. Take it, and you can have your name on the front page of the *New York Times*. Walk away, and you'll be peddling your stuff to the smallest rag in the States."

Josh sighed and let his chin fall to his chest. He wanted to be the best. When people talked about photojournalists, he wanted his name on their lips. He was young, adventurous, and dedicated to the truth of the camera—and he'd jumped in over his head by traveling so far from home. It was easy enough to follow the crowd, but he wanted to be a leader.

Without turning around, he asked, "Who do you think is coming out the back door?"

"Enrico Aragon de Manuel."

"The deposed president?" he asked incredulously, glancing over his shoulder.

"Yes."

Josh shook his head in disgust. She'd taken him for a ride. He didn't have the faintest idea why, but she had. "Everybody knows he left the country yesterday."

"Everybody knows nothing," she insisted. "My sources say he's been holed up in his bedroom and Travinas knows it."

"His bedroom?" At this, Josh turned around, letting all his disbelief show on his face. "Are you crazy?"

"Crazy like Aragon. He cut a deal with Travinas. He gave them his cabinet members in return for safe passage and a hacienda in Rio de Janeiro. While Mendez, Cavazos, and Estrada go to prison, he's going to the lap of luxury."

Her information hit him like a thunderbolt.

It also splashed his name across the front page of the *New York Times*. Dateline: San Simeon—Aragon Betrays Own Government—story and photos by Joshua Rios. It was also the first and last time he had a byline all to himself. All the succeeding ones read: Kydd and Rios. Ladies, she had insisted, always preceded gentlemen. . . .

# *Three*

Where was he? Nikki wondered, glancing up from her tattered notebook. A couple of men out of the motley crew hanging around the bar waved in greeting and she responded in kind. There had been a time when she'd avoided the other reporters covering the Latin beat. By nature they were an aggressive, wild bunch, professionally and sexually, with few scruples. But young as he was in comparison, Josh had made it clear they'd better not mess with Nikki, or with him for that matter. Her instincts hadn't let her down in her choice of a protector. Of course, Josh didn't mess around with her, either, a possibility that raced through her mind more and more often, though never as disturbingly as it had that afternoon in the jeep.

The memory brought to her face an uneasy warmth that had nothing to do with the sultry weather. She brushed her cheek with the back of her hand and shifted in her chair, returning her attention to the notebook. Josh was Josh, and she was Nikki. They were partners, business partners and friends, and both relationships were comfortable. The other possibility was a mystery she didn't have any idea of how to unravel.

"Hey, Rios," one of the reporters called. "Find anything out there today?"

"Nothing you can't read about in the *Times*." Josh's distinctly rough voice drew her attention like a magnet.

She glanced up and saw him coming out of the hotel's back door, and she felt her disconcerting blush deepen. His clothes hid the curves and angles of all the hard muscle she had memorized in bits and pieces during their months together: Josh taking his shirt off to douse himself in a mountain stream; a flash of strong legs out of her peripheral vision as he changed clothes in camp; the strength of his arms in one of the rare moments when he felt it necessary either to hold her back or hold her down. She wished she could quit thinking such crazy thoughts. They would only lead to trouble or heartache, both of which she already had in abundance.

Watching him made her wish an impossibility. Thick black hair swept back from his face, though a lock in front fell across his forehead in damp strands. Layers of the ebony silk brushed the turned-up collar of his khaki shirt. Tight jeans, worn to a soft perfection, hugged his lean hips and covered the tops of his boots. A year in the tropics had toasted his skin to a deep mahogany brown, but his eyes were still the same strange, shifting blue, and she prided herself on being able to read them like a book.

He stopped at the bar and glanced over at her, cocking his head questioningly. At her nod, he ordered two beers. She saw him pause for a minute, counting the wad of bills in his hand, then say something else to the bartender.

Curiosity, overlaid with a big dose of apprehension, pushed all the crazy thoughts out of her head as he picked up a bottle of tequila to go with the beer. Something was wrong, and her misgivings grew with every measured step he took toward the table.

She waited for him to settle into a chair before blurting out the worst possibility she could think of. "You lost the film." She would kill him if he'd lost the film.

"No," he said wearily, passing a hand across his face and peering at her over the tips of his fingers. He'd worn a hole in the carpet, pacing his room, and still he hadn't come up with the right words. Every time he'd gotten close, the image of her face had intruded. Those clear green eyes, the curve of her cheeks and brow, the soft perfection of her skin— they'd all conspired against his common sense and seduced him into giving free rein to his forbidden fantasies. All he'd accomplished in his hours alone was a frustrating state of arousal, something he'd guarded against for weeks. He felt like a fool.

"Is the typewriter acting up?" she asked, visibly relieved about the film.

"No." He reached for the tequila and poured a good two inches of it into an empty water glass. It wasn't enough, but it was a start.

"Did somebody die?" Her voice softened to a whisper as she leaned across the table, diminishing the distance between them.

Josh glanced up into her not-too-innocent eyes and felt his gut tighten. For a girl her age, she accepted death too easily. He should have gotten her out of Central America a long time ago. Pure selfishness, he thought, not liking the truth or himself.

He'd used her to achieve fame and glory—and she'd helped him get both. That she'd been using him, too, didn't ease his guilty conscience. It was time to let her go, before he used her for something else, something very personal, deeply sensual, and wrong enough to turn guilt into self-loathing.

Only in the darkest recesses of his mind did he acknowledge a fear he didn't dare voice aloud even to himself: if they made love, he might never let her go. The green-eyed witch with the young blossoming body and white-gold hair was capable of consuming him. Even now, faced with reality instead of fantasy, his body and emotions continued to dominate his nobler instincts, filling his mind with the imagined taste of her mouth, intensifying the almost painful ache between his legs. To have her just once would be a disaster. *Please, Josh, try—for one more night—to keep your brains above your belt.*

"No, Nikki, nobody has died, at least not anybody we know," he said, sliding back in his chair. A wry grin lifted a corner of his mouth as he shifted his gaze off into the night and fell silent.

Nikki never took her eyes off him. Through the long quiet moments she struggled to figure out what was going on behind the tense mask of his face. She thought she knew all of his moods, but she'd never seen him quite so strung out. Still, she felt it was best to let him take his time. Sooner or later he'd tell her what was bothering him. She reached for her beer.

"You drink too much," he said without moving an inch.

She paused with the beer halfway to her mouth, looking at him in confusion. "Well, hell, Josh. Nobody exactly recommends drinking the water."

"You swear too much, too."

"Couldn't be the company I keep," she parried lightly, trying to ignore the uneasiness edging back into her mind. Something wasn't wrong; *she* was wrong. What had she done? Was he still mad about the night before? No, she decided, he never held a grudge. Besides, she'd been right. His Spanish was atrocious. For a reporter in Central America, let alone one named Rios, not knowing the language inside out and backward was a severe handicap. How he'd grown up on the Tex-Mex border without picking up at least a smattering of the lingo was beyond her. He must have worked hard at remaining ignorant, which didn't fit in with his natural curiosity about everything else under the sun.

She barely had time to throw out her first idea before he agreed with her.

"You do keep bad company, Nikki. As a matter of fact, I can't imagine worse company than me for a seventeen-year-old girl."

"I'm eighteen, and you need to give yourself more credit, Josh." Only her smile added a teasing note to the words. The rest of her face remained coolly impassive, her eyes assessing.

He discounted the difference with a slight shrug. Then he swallowed half the glass of tequila, pulled an envelope out of his shirt pocket, and tossed it over to her side of the table.

The envelope landed softly on the rough wooden table, but the sound blocked all others from her mind. She kept her eyes glued on his, her smile fading into a grim line. She didn't need to open the envelope to know what was inside. She'd seen a hundred plane tickets.

"Dammit, Josh," she said through clenched teeth, flipping the envelope back at him. "We've been through this before, and the answer is always the same. No."

"This time it's yes." The ticket came back at her.

The simplicity of his answer unnerved her more than the hardness of his voice. He was supposed to counter with one of the dozen or so reasons he'd formulated over the last twelve months, such as her safety or her worried relatives or the completely ludicrous one about her reputation.

She picked up the envelope, then let it drop back to the table. She couldn't win playing his game.

"You wasted your money . . . as usual," she said, throwing the argument back at him, deciding to clear out all the problems at once and hopefully distract him.

Josh recognized the ploy. She'd used it many times successfully, running circles around him with convoluted logic. But not tonight. Tonight he'd win and, through the winning, lose her.

"You're going home." And she was, no matter what he did or said. The situation was out of his hands.

"I am home," she snapped impatiently. He'd picked a helluva night for a fight, she thought. They were both jumpy and tired from their run through the jungle. And he couldn't have chosen a more volatile subject if he'd searched the seven seas. He knew it, too.

Josh saw the sparks of anger in her eyes, the tightening of her mouth, and knew with a sinking heart that the end was near. He'd made her good and mad, and maybe that was for the best. Maybe in her anger she would find relief from his betrayal— for he'd betrayed her absolutely and irrevocably. He accepted what he had done, but it didn't make telling her any easier.

"Better check your passport again, Nikki." He

stalled a moment longer, wanting to hold their friendship for just a few more seconds, wanting to watch her and know she still cared enough to fight with him before she shut him completely out of her life.

Her eyes flashed with defiance. "Forget it, Josh. You can't make me go." She held her head a little higher, her shoulders a little straighter.

Her unconscious body language reminded him of all the reasons he'd kept her with him for so long. She had the courage of a person twice her age, and the purity of conviction reserved solely for the young. But it also reminded him of all the reasons he had to let her go. With the candlelight turning her hair into molten silver and her face into a sweet mystery of shadows, she broke his heart with wanting.

"Can and will," he said softly, forcing himself to hold her gaze. "The game's over, Nikki. I reported you to the authorities. They're sending an aide over in the morning to pick you up."

From one breath to the next, and the next, he watched her emotions race from shock to disbelief and finally to confusion and pain. In less than a minute, he had destroyed a year's worth of trust, a lifetime's worth of friendship.

"J-Josh?" She spoke his name in a broken whisper, offering it like a talisman against the impossible, as if the one word could hold their lives together.

He wanted to say he was sorry, but the pitiful statement didn't come close to describing his feelings. He hated the grief clouding her eyes, hated himself for putting it there, and had to look away. The next morning he would hand her over to some stuffed shirt from the embassy and then he'd get drunk and stay drunk until another story came along, or until he forgot how painfully innocent his young partner really was, how innocent she'd always been.

Nikki slowly rose from the table. His silence mocked her, the downward cast of his eyes making a sham of all they'd shared. Her body trembled, her heart beat fast and furiously, hurting, breaking, and aching all at the same time.

"Damn you," she whispered. "*Damn you.*" Then she turned and fled into the lobby.

Josh finished his beer and another double shot of tequila, all the while keeping watch on the front desk. He knew she'd make a run for it, but he also knew she wouldn't stick him with her room bill. The lady had an honest streak a mile wide. Thanks to Nikki, he had the cleanest set of books south of the border. It wasn't her fault money ran like water through his fingers.

None of his thoughts made him feel better. In fact, they made him feel a helluva lot worse. Holding his head in his hand, he poured more tequila into the glass.

Women! he thought. Who could figure them? He tried to console himself with that generality, but Nikki wasn't a generality. She wasn't even a full-grown woman. She was teasing warmth and shining brightness, and having her by his side made him special. None of the bums hanging around the bar had Nikki Kydd showing them the truth behind the obvious. None of them had Nikki complaining about their cooking with a subtle wrinkling of her nose or a grumpily voiced critical review. None of them had her sharing a campsite with them at the end of day as the tropical sun slid into the sea.

And she only looked like a full-grown woman.

"Damn." The muttered curse held merely a fraction of the frustration and anger welling inside him. He'd screwed up everything, from the minute he'd thrown the ticket at her until his last ultimate stupidity. It had all seemed so clear, so right, when he'd called the embassy. And now it all felt horrible, heart-wrenchingly horrible. His shoulders sagged in defeat.

*Big boys don't cry.* He tried another hopeless cliché and hung his head down, sighing heavily. If he started to cry, he'd know he'd had too much to drink. But he didn't feel drunk, not even close. The stricken look on her face would probably keep him stone sober until he was ninety.

Raking a restless hand through his hair, he allowed himself to consider other options. He could go to her and explain. Go to her and apologize. Go to her and—and tell her that her leaving was for the best . . . how much he cared. . . . Tell her how many nights he'd lain awake thinking of her, of the two of them. . . . Tell her he loved her, and hold her and kiss her until she believed him—and he lost his mind.

His thoughts tangled around one another until he was back in his original, overheated frame of mind. He shook his head, as if physical motion could clear away the images, but the action was useless.

With a groan of disgust, he pushed his chair back and rose to his feet. After she left, maybe he would fly down to Costa Rica for some rest and relaxation, take a vacation away from chaos. Maybe he'd find out if time really was the great healer. What was the other thing people said? Absence makes the heart grow fonder—of someone else. There was a woman in Costa Rica, a dark-haired, sloe-eyed beauty who'd made her desire obvious. In more ways than one, Nikki had put a damper on his sex life. Maybe he'd go find Gabriella what's-her-name and lose his hurt inside her.

Yeah, sure, he thought. Great idea. You're full of them, Rios. His mouth slowly tightened in pain, and his eyes squeezed shut. The mere thought of loving someone else left him feeling emptier and more alone than before. *What have you done, you stupid son of a bitch?*

Guilt and sadness overwhelmed him and he was helpless against his longings. He knew what he'd done. He'd thrown away the best thing ever to happen to him, and he couldn't let her leave feeling abandoned and betrayed. He couldn't. The year they'd shared deserved better than the bitterness she'd find to hide her pain.

He opened his eyes and let his gaze drift to the second floor of the hotel. Light shone through the slats of the shutters on the far left window, Nikki's window. Oblivious to the activity around him, he watched and waited, and soon her shadow passed into the light. Slight and fragile, her profile hung high above him in the night, hinting at her bowed head and the slender curves of her body. His fingers curled into a fist, a tight hard knot echoing the heaviness weighing down his heart.

Their time together was over. The good times, the bad times, the fighting and the running, the early morning strategy sessions, and the late night celebrations—all of them were gone. But if he reached out to her once more in friendship, maybe they could salvage the best of what they'd been.

He looked down at the tequila and reached for it, then hesitated, the sober part of him doubting his motives. Raking both hands through his hair, he held his head and struggled to put his crazy feelings in order. A wasted moment later he picked up the bottle and his glass. They'd finished a few bottles together when a story had gone bad or a source had washed out. One more bottle, shared in misery, would be a fitting end. Motives be damned. They were friends.

Walking toward the lobby, he felt a wry but weak smile curve his mouth. He'd nursed her through a few hangovers. She was a pushover when she could barely open her eyes and her head was pounding like a steel band. All in all, he'd be saving everybody, from the embassy jerk to the flight attendants, a lot of trouble if he cooled her jets before they tried to get her on the plane. Fresh, rested, and spitting mad, she might easily give them the slip—and the last thing he wanted on his conscience was Nikki Kydd roaming around the country without him. He would do a lot of things, noble or otherwise, to make sure that didn't happen.

Feeling better than he had in a week, he strode across the oak-floored lobby and bounded up the stairs two at a time.

# *Four*

Nikki slumped back against the shutters, her head down, her arms wrapped around her waist. The small balls of her fists dug into the overlarge white T-shirt hanging half off her shoulders. Tears, salty, sad, and angry, streamed down her cheeks and dampened her neck.

*Why?* The question without an answer lay heavy on her heart and mind. Why now? Why ever? They were good together. They were better than good; they were the best. Kydd and Rios had broken more stories than any of the other reporters in the whole of Central America. Kydd and Rios, not just Rios.

"Damn him," she whispered, swiping at her tears. He wasn't going to get away with his underhanded scheme, not by a long shot. She was the one who knew the countries, the politics, the culture, and she could speak Spanish around him until his head swam. She didn't need him. She didn't need him for anything.

The lie caught on the tender places of her heart, adding a razor's edge to her pain and causing a fresh wave of tears to flow. He'd used her. Josh Rios, with his dark angel face and driving ambition, had risen to the top on the sweat of her brow. And she, young and foolish, would have allowed him to go on using her. She'd given him the biggest stories of his life, and been willing to give him so much more. She'd seen how other women looked at him, with their eyes half closed and their mouths soft, and she'd known exactly what they were thinking. In her dreams, she looked at him the same way, wondering about him not as a friend but as a man.

A sob broke from her. *Damn him. Damn him. Damn him.* She pushed off the windowsill and crossed to the four-drawer dresser holding all her worldly belongings. One by one she emptied the drawers, throwing everything into the suitcase that lay open on the bed. Half the things went in; half landed on the chenille spread or on the faded rug covering the wooden floor. T-shirts and pants, all big and baggy, flew over her shoulder. Underwear and socks followed by the handful. With one clean sweep, she scooped up her shampoo, brush, sunscreen, and all the other sundries that constituted her grooming gear. She was getting the hell out of Dodge. Josh Rios could eat her dust, but he wasn't going to turn her in.

Looking down at the pitiful supply of items clutched in her arms, she felt another sob catch in her throat. Maybe if she'd fixed herself up better, maybe if she'd tried harder to look feminine, maybe then he would have seen her as more than an expendable business partner. There had been a time when she'd worn makeup and pretty clothes, but that was a lifetime ago. She'd spent a year trying to fade into the background, and she'd succeeded to the point of becoming a wallflower, a drab, shapeless wallflower.

Her pride rebelled. *No.* Josh should have looked deeper. He should have known better. He should have respected her for what she was.

Sniffling and crying, and trying not to do either, she stumbled across the small room and dumped her stuff into the suitcase. It was a mess, just like her. She sorted and arranged the clothes, trying to put them into a semblance of order. A ratty old khaki shirt here, a threadbare pair of pants there. She picked her high-top tennis shoes off the floor and held them in her hands. The shoelaces were new and bright red, the only spot of color in her wardrobe. They had been a gift from Josh.

How could he do this to her? What possible reason had she given him to call the embassy?

None. The answer finally came. None that she could accept. It was down to survival now. She was on her own again, and from here on out, she worked alone. For a moment the thought buoyed her confidence and sparked her anger back to life, but the tears didn't stop. They ran down her face, wet trails of sadness blurring her vision and catching in pools at the corners of her mouth.

*Oh, Josh. How could you?* She shoved a tennis shoe into a corner of the suitcase.

"Nikki?" Her head jerked up at the sound of his voice. He knocked and called again. "Nikki?"

"Go to hell," she cried, pulling a shirt out of the suitcase and frantically wiping her face with it. He wasn't going to catch her crying. Not her. Not Nikki Kydd.

"Nikki, please." Josh tried the door, and the knob turned in his hand. Dammit, how many times had he told her to keep her door locked? "I'm coming in."

"Go away!"

He winced as a shoe hit the wall an inch from his

face. Well, no doubt about it. She was mad. He peeked around the door, then quickly ducked. Another tennis shoe careened off the jamb, shoelaces flying.

Silently he waited for the next barrage. When nothing happened, he asked, "Are you finished?"

Only more silence answered him.

Braving all, he stepped inside, and immediately dropped the tequila to fend off a sandal. The bottle rolled off the rug and into the wall. The sandal glanced off his arm. He caught the next sandal in mid-arc, dropped it and his glass, and kept on moving forward, confident now of his safety. The lady only owned two pairs of shoes.

Nikki threw a shirt, and watched it flutter ineffectually to the floor. Her notebook came next, missing him by a mile, but unerringly finding the lamp on the dresser. The cheap porcelain base rocked once, twice, then fell with a crash, throwing the room into darkness. Josh flinched, cursed, and kept on coming.

Her choking sobs echoed through the room, and the air remained filled with shirts, pants, socks, until she was stuffing them into his arms. "Get out of here. I don't ever want to see you again. Not ever. I don't need you. I never needed you. *You* needed me. You'll see"—Her voice broke on a harsh whisper. "You'll see."

Moonshine and the glow from the outdoor lights slowly filled the room, making it impossible for her to hide her tears. She grabbed the last T-shirt out of her suitcase and found herself pressing it against the hard wall of his chest. "I—I swear, Josh Rios, you'll see."

Her fingers clenched around the thin material, pushing him away, but Josh wasn't going anywhere. He'd expected a fight—they always fought—but not this fire storm of shoes and clothes and tears. He knew her. She would regret the lamp, all two bucks' worth of it.

"I'll pay for the lamp," he said softly, feeling her hurt as deeply as his own.

"Damn right you will. Now get out of here." She dropped her hands to her sides and let the T-shirt fall. Not once did she look up at him. She didn't have the heart for looking at him.

Josh stared down at the silvery cap of her hair, the nape of her neck, the satiny sheen of her bare slender shoulder, and fell totally, helplessly in love. The breath went out of him on a ragged sigh, and he wondered what she'd say if she knew he felt like crying, too.

"Nikki, I'm sorry. I'm so sorry." He lifted his hand to touch her, but she moved away without noticing. His fingers curled, empty and cold, into his palm.

"You're worse than sorry," she whispered. "Get out, Josh. Leave."

*Leave her?* He watched her lean against the shutter over the tall window, weariness evident in the tilt of her head. Moonlight streamed in slanted lines down the length of her body, playing light and shadow along her breasts, her hips, and the silky length of her legs revealed by her shorts. He couldn't leave her. Not like this.

Drawn by invisible ties, he followed her across the room. He didn't know what to say. He didn't know what to do, but when he stood so close behind her, he automatically reached for her. His hand drifted gently along the curve from her shoulder to her neck, and this time she didn't move away. Her skin was like satin, warm and vibrant beneath his fingers and palm.

"Nikki, I want . . ." His voice trailed off, soft and husky and full of doubt.

She looked up at him, her eyes accusing and sad in the fluid band of light shining through the shutters. Tears spiked her gold-tipped lashes. Her mouth trembled, beckoning to him in all its soft sweetness. Another sigh swelled his chest.

She shouldn't have looked, Nikki thought. Looking only made leaving him harder. Pain had etched harsh lines at the corners of his mouth and darkened the depths of his eyes. A heavy sweep of ebony hair curved around his ears and lay across the collar of his rumpled khaki shirt, needing a woman's touch, a woman's caress. She wanted to smooth the worried frown from his face, starting with the tight muscles of his jaw, then sliding her fingers up to ease the tension from his brow. She'd comb through his silky black hair and caress the strong column of his neck. With a growing and oddly desperate ache, she wanted to touch him like a woman, just once. For she was leaving him tonight.

*Don't*, a warning voice cautioned, and Nikki obeyed, despite the barest pressure from his hand on her shoulder. The last thing she wanted was his pity. To save herself from doing anything foolish, she lifted her chin and whispered, "I hate you."

Josh slowly shook his head. "No, you don't," he murmured, brushing her hair back from her face. It was far too late for leaving her. Months ago, his silver-haired waif had begun weaving her magic spell around him, drawing her web ever tighter, capturing him completely. His last crazy shot at freedom had backfired. For he was there with her now, in the warmth and the darkness of the tropical night, and he wasn't letting her go.

The doubts, the rights and wrongs, faded under

his increasing need to have her. Tonight Nikki belonged to him. He'd waited so long.

With the slightest movement, he brought them
closer, his body nudging hers, his other hand sliding around her waist, fingering the narrow leather
belt holding up her shorts. "Ah, Nikki." His breath
blew softly across her cheek. "There's so little time
left. Let me stay with you tonight. Let me stay with
you . . . like this." He pressed their bodies together,
rubbing against her, letting her feel his arousal.
"Please."

Nikki froze beneath his gentle aggression, her
senses instantly alert to the new, strange pressure
of his body next to hers. She knew, and didn't know,
what his hardness meant, doubted if what she
thought she felt had anything to do with her. But
his breath was warm on her skin, teasing a path to
her ear.

"Please, Nikki," he whispered seductively, then
gently gnawed on her neck.

A thousand shooting stars burst inside her at the
tender explorations of his teeth and tongue. They
shimmered down to the tips of her fingers and settled into a heavy sweetness between her thighs.
Shocked by what he asked, by the power he had
over her, she started to back away, but his hand
immediately tightened against the small of her back.

"Don't," he commanded huskily.

"Josh, I—"

"One kiss, Nikki."

Even as he spoke, his mouth moved over hers,
and his hand swept up her neck to cup her face. His
lips brushed hers lightly, tentatively. He couldn't
force anything from her, but in his heart he knew
he didn't need force. He'd seen her eyes in unguarded
moments when she looked at him with longing. To-

night he would teach her what she'd been longing to learn and, in the teaching, heal his soul.

Finding courage in her acceptance of his chaste kiss, he opened his mouth over hers. Finally, after all these many months, he put into action the dream that had haunted his nights and slid his tongue across her lips. She tasted sweeter, felt better, than anything he'd dared imagine. His body tightened; hers softened.

Nikki's shock hit an all-time high when she realized exactly what he was doing. Josh, her Josh, was touching her as a lover, not as a friend. His mouth moved over hers and into hers repeatedly, drowning her surprise with a greater need. Of their own accord, her hands slid up his chest to grasp his shoulders. More than anything they'd shared, she wanted this kiss to remember him by, and in a hundred small ways, she told him so. She touched her tongue to his and felt his heavy sigh consume her. She pressed her hips closer, and his arms encircled her with steely strength, flexing to hold her completely. All of her thoughts, all of her senses, coalesced into one burning ambition: to touch and taste and feel Josh's body, to understand the mystery of his mouth and the way he kissed, deep and long and fully. His teeth grazed her lower lip, and pleasure rained down her body. He sucked her tongue into his mouth, and the pleasure rose again, more powerful than before. She was dying and living, and coming apart at the seams.

Josh felt her small gasps echo in his mouth, felt the rise and fall of her breasts against his chest, and he marveled at the artless ease of her response. Nikki in love was sweet, warm, wild. The night stretched out before him with a wealth of possibilities. He would love her until she'd have no other.

He'd teach her about herself in a thousand new ways, and he would teach her about him, slowly and carefully. The kiss was only a beginning, but one he never wanted to end. Her tongue tasted his lips, his mouth, and honed his arousal to a fine edge. He wanted all of her.

Groaning, he let his hand slide under her T-shirt and up around to stroke her breast. Nikki felt the heat of his palm, the gentle kneading of his fingers, and suddenly she understood what he wanted. Much more than a kiss, nothing less than everything.

A moment of panic, mixed with acute shyness, suspended her exploration of his mouth.

"Don't stop, Nikki." He breathed the words against her lips, feeling her hesitation. He rubbed his nose down the side of hers. "You're so beautiful in my hand. So warm, so full, and so mine." His husky voice strummed across her emotions, filling her with exquisite yearnings.

"I don't want to stop," she said quietly, the fall of her hair hiding her blush from him. "I don't understand, Josh. One minute you want to send me away, and the next—" Her voice softened to a whisper. "I don't know how to do this, Josh."

Only Nikki, he thought with gentle understanding, only Nikki would make such a confession. With his free hand, he lifted her chin, then let his gaze roam over the flushed beauty of her face.

"We're right together. We always have been." Using every advantage he had, he brushed his thumb over the peak of her breast and watched with pleasure as her eyes darkened with the sweetness of passion. "You must know that, Nikki."

"We've never been like this before," she said breathlessly, barely managing to keep her gaze focused on him. The sensations he sent spiraling through her body were so powerful, so new.

"We should have been, a long time ago," he said, refusing to lose her now. Physically and emotionally, he'd already started making love to her. "I can't tell you how many nights I've lain awake in the room next to yours and thought of nothing but touching you here." With his index finger, he traced the valley between her breasts.

"Oh, Josh. You don't know what you're doing to me." She felt weak and dangerously out of control.

"Yes, I do," he murmured. "You're doing the same thing to me. What you're feeling, I feel. What you want, I want. To touch and kiss and hold you naked against me until I can't even think for needing to be inside you."

The boldness of his confession singed her cheeks with embarrassment and the rest of her body with an answering need. She saw the truth of his desire in the lines of strain around his mouth. She felt it in the tense hardness of his body. She knew it in her heart.

"Why now?" she asked.

A shadow fell over his youthful face, softening the harsh angles with tender longing. "Because we're both hurting, Nikki. Because you're leaving me." His gaze was languid with the heat arcing between their bodies. "Because I love you."

She knew that, too. How could she not have known? Her love for him was so alive it colored all her days. It grew with every beat of her heart. They were so good together, how could he not love her the same way?

"Don't make me go," she whispered. *Don't make me leave you behind, where everything we've shared will fade into memories.*

"I won't forget you, Nikki. I promise. I'll come for you when I can."

A part of her died with his words. He didn't understand, and she didn't have the courage to explain. Although she would love him tonight, in the morning she would still leave him. Another love left her no choice.

How neatly the tables turned, she thought sadly, letting her gaze roam over his face. She soaked in every clean angle and tender plane, the high arch of his cheeks and the expressive curve of his lips. With the tips of her fingers, she stroked his hair, brushing it behind his ear, memorizing the silky texture, the ebony color, and the way it fell through her hand. Long after she left him, she'd remember how it felt to hold him as a woman. As she touched him, she watched his lids grow heavy, his thick lashes lower to rest on his cheeks. She loved him.

And Josh knew no one loved her more than he, not in this life, not tonight. He lowered his mouth to hers again, without any hesitation, without holding back. He plundered and tasted and teased until she was with him on every move, anticipating with him the sweet mysteries still to be explored. He felt her breath catch as he slipped her T-shirt off her shoulders, heard her low moan as he unbuttoned his shirt and gathered her close, bringing her breasts against the warmth of his chest.

His muscles tightened. His heart beat with even greater force. Nikki was his, and he gave free rein to the sweet ache growing in his loins, letting his feelings pour out of him.

Nikki arched against him. His body was satin-sheathed steel, hard muscle and sinew covered with warm, dark skin. He felt like heaven to touch. She pushed his shirt off his shoulders and felt his hands on the buckle of her belt. Never once did he stop kissing her.

Garment by garment, their clothing fell to the floor, his shirt following her T-shirt, his jeans following her shorts. Both belt buckles clattered against the wood planks in a muted counterpoint to their soft moans and sighs. When they were both stripped to their underwear, Josh felt a mental hesitation that in no way stopped him from sliding his hand beneath her panties. This was her first time, he reminded himself even as he caressed the silky skin below her waist. *Her first time.* The implications suddenly became clear, and just short of his destination, he retreated.

But he didn't stop kissing her. His mouth devoured hers hungrily, priming her for the boldness of his next move. Holding the nape of her neck with his palm, he lifted her deeper into the kiss and slowly urged her hand down the front of his body. It was quite possible that his soon-to-be-lover had no idea what she was getting herself into.

Her fingers trailed delicately down his chest, his abdomen, and farther, until his breath caught in a groan.

"That's what you do to me, Nicolita, what you've been doing to me for months." He buried his face in the golden veil of her hair, reveling in her tentative exploration and the fireworks she set off with her touch. At her soft whisper in his ear, he chuckled, low and throatily. "Don't worry. We'll be a perfect fit. I promise." With another bold move, he pushed her panties off her hips and down her legs, then began his own sweet exploration.

The heat and humidity of the night closed around them like a sultry cocoon as they stretched out on the bed, naked in each other's arms. He used his hands and mouth a hundred different ways on her body, turning her into fire and flame, bringing her to the brink of release and easing her back down. He didn't want her frightened by the intense emotions and sensations of a lover's climax, but he definitely wanted her to climax. Her arousal was paramount in his mind, for some admittedly selfish reasons. He wanted to feel her release wash over him. He wanted to love her and know she felt everything he felt. He wanted to share this night completely, to make her feel her body in all its exquisite perfection, to leave a brand upon her heart that no other could erase.

Nikki shimmered and arched under his sweet, relentless torture, loving him in return, learning how to make his pleasure last, how to draw her tongue across his mouth and her hands down his body until he had to make her stop.

"Please," he begged, his fingers tightening around her wrists. "Give me a chance. I don't want to hurt you."

"You had your chance a year ago, Rios," she murmured close to his ear. She loved the feel of his body, slick and hot, over hers, and wanted him, as he'd promised, deep inside her. "You could have walked away." The last was a bare whisper against his throat. She adjusted her hips, silently telling him of her readiness and the desperate need consuming her.

"Not then," he said huskily. "And not now, but I've got to have some cooperation or I'm going to—"

"You're not going to hurt me, Josh. Not now, not unless you stop." She wrapped one silky leg around his hips, and instantly unraveled his last tenuous hold on control.

Clenching the sheets in his hands, he covered her mouth with his own and tried to hold himself back.

Instead he found himself slipping inside her, every moment becoming more urgent.

Nikki gasped, and felt the world open up like a flower's petals rising to meet the sun. He filled her completely and still took her higher, beyond any realm of sensation she'd imagined. Each thrust of his body weakened her hold on reality. She held him tighter and tighter, reaching for an elusive pinnacle, a pinnacle he took her to when he slipped his hand between their bodies and touched her with a rhythmic, intimate caress. Then she was tumbling down in rippling waves of eternity, hearing her name whispered over and over in her ear. The end was sweet and long, lasting forever, tying her irrevocably to one man.

Spent, sated, and filled with wonder, Josh collapsed on top of her. Never, ever, would he let her go. He rubbed his face in the creamy valley of her breasts, kissing each in turn, worshiping the woman who had exploded all his myths of love, turning them into ashes compared to the reality of loving her. No matter what he'd said or done earlier, in the morning he knew he would be down on his knees with his heart in his hands, begging her to stay.

Nikki ran her fingers through the tangled strands of his hair, holding her tears inside. One taste of such magic would never be enough, not for a lifetime. No random chance had given her Joshua Rios. They were meant to be together.

"I love you, Josh." The words were spoken softly to hide the catch in her throat.

He heard it anyway. He lifted his head and gently eased out of her body. "Don't cry, Nikki, please." He kissed her lips, her cheeks, her brow. "I love you. Don't cry." With consummate care, he reassured her of his love, his presence, his desire to hold her and always keep her safe.

But in the silent dark hours before dawn, after he'd loved her again and while he slept peacefully in her arms, she found the strength to slip away from his side.

Quietly she dressed and repacked her suitcase, picking her clothes up off the floor. Then, with only one longing, loving backward glance, she closed the door behind her—and locked it to keep him safe.

# *Five*

Summer heat lay over San Simeon like a steaming blanket, smothering the normal hustle and bustle of the city night. Nikki sat at her desk in front of the open French doors leading to her apartment balcony. Humidity and her own sweat soaked her cotton T-shirt and shorts, but she barely noticed the oppressive weather. Her life had started to unravel seven hours ago, and she'd been running at breakneck speed ever since, trying to salvage the remnants.

Three years almost to the day, she thought. Please, Josh, remember. Please remember.

She typed frantically, pounding the keys of her small manual typewriter, hating herself for every subtly worded phrase designed to bring him back to her. She didn't even know where he was. His own editor didn't know. Still somewhere in South America, he'd guessed. Josh's latest stories had come out of Colombia, but with the last one he'd requested a few weeks off. She only prayed that wherever he was, he was still reading the newspapers. His life, and her mother's life, depended on it.

A dazzling array of candles flickered around her desk, dripping wax into their platters. Her computer sat uselessly on a file cabinet, a slave to the electricity San Simeon seemed incapable of providing in reliable quantities. The whole country was plunging into chaos again, but this time Nikki was determined not to go down with it.

A voice crackled on the phone tucked between her shoulder and ear. She immediately stopped typing and covered her other ear with her free hand.

"Hello? Hello?"

"Your call is . . ." The operator's voice trailed off in static.

"Dammit," she muttered.

"I beg your pardon?"

"Nikki?"

"David!" Nikki sighed with relief.

"Collect call from Nikki Kydd. Will you accept—"

"I accept!" David yelled into the phone.

"David, I've got the story of the century breaking here," Nikki said in a rush. "Strictly front page, and a guaranteed twelve-hour lead on everybody else in this godforsaken country."

"That's what I pay you the big bucks for."

Normally she would have taken the opportunity to try to wrangle a raise out of him, not that she'd get it. David had a line of bull a mile long about budget restrictions at the *Washington Post*. But the only thought on her mind was the deal Travinas had offered her.

"I want you to take a very light hand on this, David," she said, working to keep the desperation out of her voice. "*Very light*. Print it the way I give it to you and I promise to stay out of trouble for the rest of the year." It was an easy promise to make. If her editor ever found out about the message she had hidden in the article, she'd lose her job and he would never have to worry about her again. Neither would any other editor working for a respectable newspaper in the States.

"You always ask for the moon, Nikki." He sounded leery.

"This time I want the whole Milky Way, and you'll be happy to give it to me. Listen to this." She whipped the top sheet of paper off the pile next to her typewriter. " 'Intrigue and betrayal remain the watchwords of politics in San Simeon. In two surprise moves on Thursday, General Travinas followed in the footsteps of his predecessor, Enrico Aragon de Manuel, by imposing martial law and disbanding his own cabinet. Included in the purge was the minister of economic development, Carlos Delgado, a man many consider Travinas's most dangerous opponent.' "

"It's only Wednesday night," David said.

"And we've got an exclusive."

"Where did you get this story?"

"From Travinas, this afternoon."

"How?"

"I sold my soul," she answered truthfully. Travinas had given her no other choice. Her mother's freedom for Joshua Rios, he'd said bluntly. Nikki didn't know what in the hell Josh was up to, but he'd suddenly become the hottest commodity in San Simeon—if she could get him back in the country. "Come on, David. Get me a typist. Let's go with this. Check my track record if you have trouble sleeping tonight. I've never been wrong. You know that."

"I'd hate for this to be the first time."

"It's not," she stated emphatically.

"Okay, Nikki. You sold me."

"Thanks."

Half an hour later Nikki hung up the phone and slumped over her typewriter, every muscle in her body aching with tension. There was no turning back now. She'd set the wheels in motion; she just prayed they wouldn't go spinning out of control.

A deep sob caught in her throat. Damn Travinas. She'd never felt more manipulated in her life. She'd been sidestepping his deportation threats for so long, she'd never considered the possibility that he might have a use for her. Well, he'd found two—emotional blackmail and betrayal of the best friend and only lover she'd ever had. He wanted Joshua Rios at any cost.

In his palatial office, he'd torn her values apart piece by piece, stealing every shred of her integrity and reducing her to a helpless mass of conflicting loyalties and loves. Her mother's freedom, the remaining years of her life, in exchange for getting Josh back into San Simeon. She'd had a choice: accept Travinas's proposal and pray she could come up with the right solutions at reckoning time, or play the saint and reject the offer out of hand.

Nikki knew she wasn't a saint, but she'd always thought there were a few sacrosanct lines she would never cross. Then Travinas had shown her a photograph of her mother. One look had convinced her there was more at stake than a person's freedom. The woman in the picture was near death, not only in spirit but in body as well. Empty eyes had stared back at Nikki from a hollow, haggard face. Four years of imprisonment had changed Helen Cavazos from a pampered matron of society into an ancient, withered woman without hope. But the general had a much worse fate in mind for Josh; he'd sicced the mad dog Brazia on his trail.

Even in the relative safety of her apartment, the

memory of Travinas's words sent a shudder of fear through her body: "I will have Joshua Rios, Señorita Kydd, with or without your help. Brazia left for Colombia yesterday. Unfortunately, Rios had already disappeared. It could take Brazia weeks to track your friend down, and I don't have weeks to wait. I have already made you a generous offer for your help, but if you need added incentive to overcome your naive aversion to betrayal, think of this—if Rios proves difficult or is reluctant to return, Brazia will kill him. I will lose some important information if he does, but I can still win the war. And winning, señorita, is the only thing that matters."

"Damn him!" She brushed back frightened tears as she jerked open the top desk drawer and pulled out her address book. Travinas hadn't wanted to give her the story, but she'd convinced him that the front page of the *Post* was the quickest, most reliable way of contacting Josh, and she'd known the general had something big planned. The whole country was growing restless, waiting for the ax to fall. Travinas's final willingness to give her what she wanted had confirmed Josh's unprecedented importance.

Now she was going to use that information to her advantage in every conceivable way. Yes, she'd promised him Josh, but she wasn't going to lead Josh to slaughter. Not if Carlos Delgado appreciated the early warning, and not if she could convince the minister of Josh's value.

But the biggest "if" of all was Josh. Would he remember? Would he understand the hidden message? And if he did understand, would he care enough to come? The love they'd shared had been fleeting, barely a memory now, but their friendship had been inviolate—until the night he betrayed her.

Nikki slid back in her chair and covered her face with her hands. *Please come, Josh. Please come back to me . . . and when this is over, please forgive me.*

Mustache or no mustache? Josh leaned forward over the sink and eyed the sleek line of whiskers above his mouth. Bright Panamanian sunshine streamed through the bathroom window, warming his shower-damp skin. Morning birds chirped and sang in the mango trees edging the courtyard of his rented bungalow. He whistled along with them as he tied a towel around his waist.

A few more weeks and he'd have a regular set of handlebars, he thought, but he went ahead, lifting the scissors and starting to cut. The mustache had served its purpose. It had turned him from Josh Rios into Juan Alonso for the week necessary to track down the last informant he needed to bring General Travinas to his knees. Lord, what a sordid life the bastard had led.

A knock on the door stopped him in mid-snip. "Señor Rios?"

"Come on in, Quico," Josh hollered over his shoulder, recognizing the teenager's voice. "Go ahead and put it all on the patio table. Did you find the newspapers?"

"Did I find them yesterday morning? And the morning before that? Did I find them last week?"

Josh grinned into the mirror. The boy was getting cheeky. "Yes, you found them last week, but I wasn't here yesterday or the day before. I'll never know if you found those papers."

"But, señor, I put them right—" He stopped suddenly, realizing Josh was teasing him. "They are right where I put them, on your bedside table, and from the mess they are in, I would guess you also found them, maybe even slept with them."

Josh chuckled. "What's for breakfast?"

"Your favorite. Coffee and sweet rolls, *pan dulce.*" Quico's voice faded as he walked out to the patio.

"And what's happening in the world?" Josh raised his voice as he lathered his face.

"Trouble. Always trouble." Quico walked back through the open doors, carrying one of the newspapers.

"Anyplace in particular?"

"In America everybody is getting richer, some people too rich. You're throwing them in jail. Strange kind of trouble." He paused for a moment, scanning the front page. "No more trouble in Panama, but San Simeon has big trouble, very big trouble."

Josh stopped shaving and slowly lowered his razor to the sink. "What paper is that?" He wiped the shaving cream off his face.

"The *Post.*"

"Let me see it. Go get the *Times.*" He took the paper and sat down on the edge of the bathtub. The headline had him swearing under his breath: "Travinas Declares Martial Law, Ousts Cabinet." The front page byline was painfully predictable—Nikki Kydd—and the dateline told him the story had broken the day after he'd gone searching for his underground informant. The damn thing was four days old, and he was sitting in Panama.

Quico came rushing back in with the *Times.*

"Forget it," Josh said. He didn't need any more old news. He reached into the pocket of the pants hanging on the towel rack and pulled out a wad of bills. He shoved them into Quico's hand. "Go get all the local papers, today's edition and yesterday's if you can find them. Go quickly."

Josh watched the boy disappear through the courtyard, then returned his attention to the newspaper. He skimmed the article, getting angrier with each successive paragraph. Somewhere in the back of his mind he wondered if Travinas had somehow gotten wind of the story he'd been working on for the last three years. The truth was enough to panic anybody into cracking down, especially if that truth was grade A blackmail material in unfriendly hands. A lot of the people Josh had dealt with wanted revenge against Travinas, but any one of the few who didn't might have decided to play both sides against the middle by telling the general a man named Rios was digging into his past.

Under those conditions, Josh wouldn't give two bits for the value of his life in San Simeon. Luckily he didn't need to return to San Simeon. A man in Panama had given him the final details of Travinas's cryptic history.

But his anger had another, deeper cause, one that he couldn't control, had never been able to control. Nikki Kydd, the young woman whose love and betrayal had marked his turning point from a boy into a man. There had never been another like her, and she was still neck deep in the hottest water in Central America.

Remembered pain tightened his mouth into a grim line. The weeks he'd spent looking for her had left permanent scars on his heart. The long days filled with dead ends, the even longer nights of fear, had turned his carefree existence into a battleground where hope always lost out to reality. He'd left messages in a dozen of the places he'd expected her to go, but she had kept running and he hadn't been able to catch her. In the end her total rejection of him as a friend, a partner, and a lover had forced him to leave San Simeon. Leave or go crazy.

Three years later, the choice was still clear in his mind. He focused again on the newspaper in his hands. Three years later, she still had the power to wound.

He read the article again, more slowly this time. The story unfolded line after line, speaking to him on a personal as well as a political and journalistic level. Nikki was good, the best. Despite her intense hatred of Travinas, she kept to the facts.

But by the second reading, those facts started to unravel a bit around the edges. Everything was in place, almost too neatly. His eyes narrowed, and he pulled a washcloth off the sink, using it to wipe away a stray dab of soap. Beginning at the top, he combed through the story again, searching for the details causing him unease. He found one in the second column, in a quote from a minor official, or so the article said. Josh recognized the name for another reason. The man, or a man with the same name, had been a friend of theirs. He'd owned a cantina they'd frequented, and Josh doubted if the congenial saloon keeper had switched loyalties and become one of Travinas's followers.

Coincidence, he decided, in spite of his natural journalistic aversion to coincidence. But two paragraphs down he found another memory-jolting sentence, and one more in the next column. The wording in all of them was subtle, the implication almost imperceptible, yet as he read the lines again, the hint of a plea became clear.

Plea for what? And to whom? Nikki was too careful a writer for the hidden meaning to be a result of sloppy work. She'd been sending a message to someone. Only that person—and another who knew her as well as he did himself—would understand.

A knot of fear slowly formed in his gut, making it impossible for him to concentrate. In disgust, he strode into the bedroom and tossed the paper on the bed. He was overreacting, seeing mysteries where none existed. He'd be better off if he, too, kept to the facts. He had only two: she was still in San Simeon and the country was falling down around her ears.

He grabbed his pants and walked over to the dresser for clean underwear. Over the years he'd followed her career through half a dozen newspapers until she'd landed a permanent position at the *Post*. He'd sent her a card, in a fit of weakness, the first time she made the front page, but she hadn't replied, or if she had, the letter had never reached him. Now Nikki Kydd did only front-page stories.

He zipped his pants, then almost resentfully picked up the paper and snapped it open. Leaning over the nightstand, he underlined the statements he thought could be part of a message, and he felt more like a fool with every stroke of his pen. Until he put them all together.

He wasn't imagining things. Nikki was sending a message, and she was sending it to him. Slowly he sank down on the bed, the paper spread between his knees. The message spoke of trouble, of need, of a friendship she'd never forgotten, and if he twisted the words ever so slightly, maybe also of love.

He lowered his chin to his chest and closed his eyes. He'd missed her for so long, and now she wanted him back. He shook his head, the hint of a wry smile lifting a corner of his mouth. She sure had lousy timing.

Quico came running back in from the patio, a half

a dozen papers in his arms. "I found them all, Josh. Today's and yesterday's."

Josh looked up, then checked his watch. "No time now, *amigo*. Stuff them in my satchel and go ask your mama how much I owe her."

"You're leaving?" Disappointment stopped the boy in his tracks.

" 'Fraid so. I've got a long overdue date with a lady."

"A woman?" Quico asked, as if that was a most unacceptable reason for leaving a good buddy.

A woman? Josh repeated silently. He didn't really know. In some ways she'd been old beyond her years, even at seventeen and eighteen, and the night she'd made love with him had transcended any and all boundaries of age or experience. But to leave him without a word? He didn't know if that had been the act of a frightened girl or a calculating woman. It was time to find out.

# *Six*

The city was coming apart at the seams, seething with revolt and defiance. Fires burned in the barrio, their flames brightening the night sky to the east of the Plaza District. Any day now, Nikki knew the fires would be burning right outside the Paloma Grand Hotel, the smoke blackening the white marble columns and darkening the view from her second floor apartment. The crowds were already spilling into the downtown area, armed with rocks and slogans.

Honking her horn and swearing in short bursts, she maneuvered her Chevy through the throng of people in the street. Three days in the jungle had left her in no mood to do vehicular battle. She was exhausted, emotionally and physically, running on empty in all departments except for an overabundance of nervous energy. Two blocks from the Paloma, she gave up on driving and pulled over to the curb. She'd have to walk.

The moment she stopped, a rock bounced off the hood of the car. She flinched at the thudding sound, feeling her first pang of fear. Damn Delgado for keeping her hanging around Sulaco all day. She should have left the northern village where he was holed up early that morning. She should have been home long before the nightly riots began, but he'd made it clear from the beginning that if she wanted to deal with him, it would be on his terms and on his schedule. He had a country to claim.

Without any facts to back her up, and despite his gratitude for her warning phone call, she'd had a difficult time convincing him that it was in his best interest to make sure nothing happened to Joshua Rios. But she'd done it. She had all of her players in place: her mother on the brink of freedom; Travinas pacing his office day in and day out, waiting for word of Josh's arrival; and Delgado ready to use his men to cover the supposed hostage exchange and ensure everyone's safety. The only player missing was Josh. Her week-long attempts to contact him through his newspaper had resulted in nothing. No one knew where he was, but neither had there been any news of his death.

Nikki reached over to the passenger seat and slipped the strap of her duffel bag over her shoulder. She sat for a moment, eyeing the moving crowd and waiting for a break. When it came, she got out of the car and was immediately swept into the mass of shouting humanity.

Josh stood in the shadows at the south end of the Paloma's entrance. For two days he'd been watching the hotel, calling her apartment, and keeping a low profile, all the while fighting the sinking feeling that he was too late. If she didn't show up that night, he'd have to blow his cover and start some serious looking. He didn't dare wait any longer if she was in trouble, because nobody he'd ever met knew more about getting into trouble than Nikki Kydd.

The crowd pressed up to the hotel's portico, and he had to struggle to hold his ground. Someone stepped on his foot. Another man fell against his back. Josh swore at each accidental assault, but when a sharp elbow caught him in the side, he reacted instinctively, grabbing the thin arm and wrenching it backward. Only the man's stricken face kept him from perpetrating his own accident and breaking the bone.

With a muttered curse, he released the man into the receding crowd. His nerves were raw from waiting and worrying. He reached inside his satchel and pulled a cheroot out of a thin metal case, a habit he'd picked up the last time he'd been looking for her. He struck a match on the stone wall at his back.

Inhaling deeply, he returned his gaze to the hotel entrance, then searched the street. The cloud of smoke caused him to squint, impairing his vision for a moment, but when it cleared he saw her. His cupped hands still in front of him; his breath caught in his throat.

*Nikki* . . . Her name whispered across his mind. Feelings he thought he had controlled welled up inside him, sharper and more painful than his memories. Not taking his eyes off her, he drew in a slow, deep breath. He should have come back for her a long time ago, a long, long time ago.

The match burned down to his fingers, and with a soft curse, he dropped it on the ground. When he looked up, she had disappeared.

"Dammit," he muttered, throwing down the cheroot and plunging into the mob.

Nikki stumbled along with the crowd, getting jostled and jolted. If she didn't come up with a quick move soon, she'd end up in front of the palace or, more likely, in front of a barricade of riot-control troops—and those were the up-side possibilities. On the down side, she could end up trampled to death.

In the way of unruly masses, the mob heaved to the right, bringing her closer to the Paloma. Nikki made her break, shoving through the cordon of men surrounding her, and was shoved right back. A blow to her shoulder made her grimace with pain. She tightened her mouth and kept pushing. Suddenly a hand circled her wrist and jerked her sideways. She stumbled, but the hand kept her from falling, and the relentless grip kept her moving toward the Paloma, pulling her ever closer to the tall man making an opening through the crowd. In seconds she was under the protection of his arm.

She held her duffel close to her chest and wrapped her other hand around the man's belt, clinging to her free ride. His long, powerful legs strode forcefully forward. She matched her steps to his, stretching her own stride, feeling his thigh moving against hers and his heavy boots coming down next to her tennis shoes.

Half a minute later, he'd accomplished the impossible. He'd gotten her free of the worst of the crowd. She glanced up with words of gratitude on her lips, but they died instantly, replaced by a gasp of disbelief.

Josh looked down at her, a small grin twisting his mouth despite his grim expression. His arm tightened around her shoulders as he fought their way back toward the Paloma, pushing through the yelling, shoving men. At the side entrance to the hotel's garden courtyard, he ducked under an iron-grilled archway and swept her around in his arms, so her back was against the high adobe wall.

The sounds of the riot faded to a rumbling backdrop, softened by the intensity of his gaze. He stared at her for a long moment, towering over her, his chest heaving as hard as her own. Then he cupped her face in his hands and slowly lowered his forehead to rest on hers. He held her, his thumbs tracing the contours of her cheeks.

A thousand emotions collided in her heart as her eyes drifted closed. Only the wall and his touch kept her knees from buckling with shock. Their breath mingled in soft gasps for air. He'd come back to her. Against the odds, he'd evaded Brazia's deadly grasp and returned to her. The last of her nervous energy drained out of her with the weakness of relief.

Josh felt her shuddering sigh in the pressure of her breasts rising against his chest. Her skin was soft, and damp from the humid air, her hair a mass of tangled silk around his fingers. He'd missed her. Lord, how he'd missed her. Without a word he tilted her head back and let his mouth slide down to hers, teasing his memories of love back to life.

The sweet invasion stole her last coherent thought, left her helpless, caught in a trap of unexpected tenderness. Her hands met at the back of his neck, her fingers tunneling through the hair lying across his collar. He groaned and pressed her harder against the garden wall.

The overpowering strength of him swept her further from reality. She clung to him out of need. He'd come back to her as a lover, not as a friend, and until that moment she hadn't realized how desperately she needed both. She had been alone so long.

"Nikki, Nikki," he whispered, kissing the side of her nose, the corners of her lips. Then he slipped his tongue inside her mouth to taste the rich sweetness that was hers alone.

He'd made a mistake. Josh knew that the instant her lips parted and sent a shaft of desire spiraling through his body. The longing for her had been pent up for too many years, through too many sleepless nights. His hands slid down to her breasts, then back up under her arms, lifting her higher against him. He wanted everything she had to give, everything she'd given him once—the mindless passion, the complete forgetting of self and the finding of each other. He wanted to discover the woman inside the girl he'd loved.

He wanted to unbutton her shirt and slip his hand inside. But now was not the time, and the Paloma garden wasn't a safe place to linger, not with her body and her every touch distracting him beyond reason. Reluctantly, he tore his mouth away, ending the kiss with a soft groan.

"Dammit, Nikki." His voice broke with concern, and he lifted his hands to her shoulders. "What were you doing out there? Trying to make the front page with an obituary?"

"No," she whispered, barely making a sound, her heart beating wildly against his.

"Where have you been? I've been here for two days, trying to avoid half the San Simeon National Security Force. The hotel is crawling with NSF cops. Why?"

Confusion clouded her eyes. "The Paloma is being watched?" Breathlessly she parted her lips and slid her hands down to rest against his chest, straining his control.

He removed his hands from her shoulders and braced himself against the adobe wall, forcing himself not to reach for her again. "Around the clock.

Four men on every shift. Answer my other questions." He had to know what was going on before he
made another move.

"I've been in Sulaco, and I . . . I don't know," she
answered. Yes, she thought, he had kissed her, but
it hadn't taken him long to get down to business. She
didn't know what to make of the lightning-fast
change, but she knew her lips were still warm from
his mouth. She knew every time his heart beat beneath her palm.

"Did I miss something in the message?" he asked.
"Was I supposed to meet you in Sulaco?"

"No, I—" She stumbled in midthought, unsure of
what to say next.

"Then why were you there?"

"A . . . a man," she stammered.

He said something obscene, glancing away. His
eyes came back to her, darkened by the night and
the unmistakable anger suddenly hardening his voice.
"That's a hell of an answer, Nikki. What kind of
man? Your lover?"

Lover? What was he talking about? Her confusion
increased, and she lowered her gaze to the ground.
She needed a minute, just a minute, to catch her
breath, to believe he was really there, to figure out
what was going on with his rapid-fire interrogation.
Lord, she wished he hadn't kissed her like that. It
made everything so much more complicated.

Josh didn't miss the evasive glance, and it did
little to lighten his mood. He'd thought about her
taking another lover too many times not to believe it
now. The idea had prompted more than one drunken
binge that first year, and a few since. She'd been
his, and he'd thrown her away.

Damn her for asking him there for half a reason—
and damn himself for believing there was more. He

pushed away from the wall, putting some distance between them. "Do they still leave the back door to this place unlocked?" He wouldn't be making any more mistakes.

"Yes," she said weakly, trying not to reach for him again, to reassure herself of his presence. For a moment she'd felt safe in his arms, the only moment of security she'd had in many days.

"Then let's get inside where we can talk. I think you've got a helluva lot of explaining to do." He grabbed her arm and roughly pulled her behind him, barely controlling his anger. The woman had a lot of nerve asking him there when she had another lover. Too much nerve for even the infamous Nikki Kydd to get away with.

Given no choice, Nikki ran with him, following him deeper into the garden. Palm trees and hibiscus crowded together in the narrow alley leading from the street to the lushly overgrown grounds nestled between the wings of the hotel. He didn't slow his pace when they entered the courtyard, but he did veer off the path, skirting the flowering hedge. Close to the rear entrance, he stopped and crouched down, pulling her with him.

"Did you tell anybody I was coming back to San Simeon?" he asked even before she regained her balance.

"No." The white lie fell from her lips without thought. She had hoped he'd come, prayed he'd come, but she hadn't *known* he'd come.

"Have you done anything to get yourself in trouble with the NSF?"

"I don't think so."

"Then I take it they're just a complication and nothing personal?"

He was moving too fast for her, his questions

coming too quickly. She closed her eyes, trying to concentrate, but all she could think about was that he'd come back to her, kissed her crazy, then gotten so mad he couldn't see straight.

"What's the matter?" he asked. "Are you hurt?"

"Dammit, Josh," she whispered, reaching the end of her rope. "Don't play the investigative reporter with me, and why should you care how many cops—" She stopped abruptly, realizing the stupidity of her question and the foolishness of the anger that had prompted it. Travinas had virtually put a price on his head, and although Josh didn't know about the price or what it was, he knew he wasn't safe in San Simeon. What he didn't know was that he wasn't safe anywhere, not with Brazia on his tail.

Time. There wasn't enough time to persuade him to play the game her way. He'd never been a good follower, and the last thing she needed was another adversary. There were too many possibilities for disaster in her intricately pieced puzzle, too many volatile personalities, too many conflicting goals. Two days and the whole thing would be over. Then he could hate her for the rest of his long life.

"What's the matter, Nikki?" His voice broke into the silence, and his hands tightened on her arms as he gave her a small shake.

"Nothing." She took a deep breath. "I don't want to argue with you. Thanks for coming. I'll never forget that you came when I needed you."

"Yeah, be sure to tell your Sulaco boyfriend." He released her and turned back toward the entrance. "Looks clear to me. Do you see anything?"

She opened her mouth to explain away his misunderstanding, then immediately shut it again. A "boyfriend" in Sulaco might be a handy addition to her mixed bag of half-truths and lies. "I don't see anything from here. Let me go first and check the stair-well." If this was going to be her game—and it *was*—then she had to take full responsibility. No more falling into his arms. She had to stay sharp, on top of everything. She wouldn't add inadvertent seduc-tion to her list of crimes.

"No way." He reached for her hand. "We'll do this together. If somebody is in there, I don't want them grabbing you. And if there's somebody out here, I don't want them grabbing you either."

His concern unleashed a fresh wave of doubts, leaving her as disconcerted as his kiss had. She would never make it like this. She'd been alone too long. More than the memories of his lovemaking, the memories of his friendship had haunted her nights. They'd been so good together. "I've missed you, Josh," she whispered, allowing herself one final weakness.

In the slightest of gestures, his thumb stroked down the length of hers. "Yeah," he drawled huskily. "I've missed you, too."

Luck was with them as they made their way up the back stairs of the old hotel. The little-used stair-well was dark, the railing rickety. Nikki felt her way along the wall until they reached the second floor landing. Taking the lead again, Josh checked the hall before he allowed her to walk down it to her apartment. When she had the door open, he joined her, quickly stepping inside.

She reached for the light switch, but his hand over hers stopped her from turning it on.

"Wait," he commanded.

For an instant she thought he was going to kiss her again, and she steeled herself to reject him. Instead he strode across the living room and drew the drapes on the French doors leading to the balcony.

"Okay, you can flip on the lights." He bent and turned on a lamp on her desk. Subdued light spilled from beneath the shade, revealing his rumpled and travel-stained clothing, and a man much different from the boy she'd left, asleep and beautiful, tangled in the sheets where he'd shared his love.

He looked older and harder than she remembered, more worn, his eyes more cautious, and he looked unbelievably good to her. Dark hair swept back from his face and feathered across his collar in shaggy layers, untouched by a barber's hand for many weeks. His skin was still burned brown except for the thin scar tracing his temple, but the faint lines at the corners of his eyes had deepened.

The wide strap of a military-style satchel angled across his chest, a gray band against his faded dark shirt. Black canvas pants hung low on his hips and broke across a pair of scuffed hiking boots that looked as if they'd seen many miles. She remembered him not quite as thin, not quite as rough around the edges, and somewhere in the back of her heart, she knew he, too, had been alone for a long time.

"The lights, Nikki," he repeated softly. He'd felt her gaze roam over him like a touch, and he wanted to see her, wanted to see the woman he'd missed in so many ways through so many nights. He wanted to see the face that came to him in his dreams.

"Yes, of course." She flipped the switch and the light flooded over her, transfixing her in a pool of brilliance.

He held her eyes for a moment, then turned his head, taking in her apartment. "I had to twist your editor's arm to get your address out of him. You forgot to tell him I was okay." A grin curved his mouth, yet didn't quite reach his eyes.

"I'm sorry," she said, turning aside and laying her duffel bag on the counter dividing the kitchen from the living room. She had forgotten to tell David to give Josh Rios any information he requested, and if she'd forgotten that, what else had she forgotten? With shaky hands, she pulled the bandanna from around her neck and used it to mop her face. The heat in the closed-up apartment was stifling, and even two combined suites didn't seem big enough to hold the two of them and her memories. "Thanks again for coming. I was afraid you wouldn't get the message, or that you wouldn't remember."

"I remember everything up until the night you left. Things got a little hazy for a while after that." The barest touch of condemnation crept into his voice. He tried to keep it out, really tried, the way he tried to force a smile onto his face. But it hurt to look at her, standing there with her hair falling down around her shoulders and her pretty face flushed.

She'd changed little over the years. Her hair was longer, her delicate features a shade more clearly defined, but her mouth still hinted at the sweet passion he'd found with her on a sultry summer night. The slender curves of her body still beckoned to him like a promise. It took every ounce of will-power he had not to walk over and pull her back into his arms.

"I'm sorry," she said again, her voice hoarse with regret.

"Yeah." He pulled a fresh cheroot out of the case, then lifted the satchel strap over his head and dropped the bag on the couch. He'd wanted to see her, and now he had.

So much for the reunion, he thought, his jaw

tight. With a flick of his wrist, he struck a match off his pants.

Surprised, she asked, "When did you start smoking?"

"About . . . three years . . . ago," he said between puffs. His eyes met hers over the flame, daring her to ask him why.

He was angry, still so angry about the past, she thought, amazed. She didn't say a word when he dropped the burned match into her crystal candy dish.

"Okay, Nikki. Tell me why I'm here."

No polite inanities preceded his demand—no "how have you been" and, thankfully, no "why did you leave." He wanted the facts, his "helluva good explanation." Last chance, Nikki, she thought. She did a light-speed search of her heart and didn't come up with even a shred of the courage it would take to tell him the truth. Deception it would be, the safety of deception.

"Travinas has offered me a deal," she began, then paused to swallow hard. The bandanna was a twisted ball of damp cotton in her hands. "I need your help to pull it off." She stopped, watching him carefully for any sign of a reaction.

"Go on," he said with a calmness he was far from feeling. The mention of the general's name hit him like a hard punch to the stomach. Nikki and Travinas. In his mind the combination spelled certain catastrophe.

"He regrets breaking off diplomatic relations with the United States, and now he wants back in, but on very limited terms." Days of practice kept the lies moving off her lips, smoothly if not easily. "He doesn't want anyone in his government to know what he's doing. He's only interested in setting himself up in case he loses San Simeon."

"What's he offering you?"

"He'll release my mother before he leaves." She stood absolutely still, afraid to look away from him.

"And what's he offering me?"

"Nothing. You're my idea, and I'll give you exclusive rights to the story when it breaks." Come on, Josh, she prayed, buy it. Let me keep this as simple as possible, so I don't go under, so I don't screw everything up and get us all hurt.

"Why? What do you need me for?"

"You reported the Washington beat for a while. You must have connections." He hadn't so much as raised an eyebrow since she'd started, and that made her very nervous.

"A few," he agreed. "But your editor lives there. I met David a couple of times, and believe me, he's loaded with State Department connections."

"This is personal for me, not business. All I care about is getting my mother out, and I don't want to be pressured by anyone with a different agenda." A tiny bead of sweat ran down the side of her face, forcing her to untangle her fingers from the bandanna. She dabbed at her face while he watched her.

"Then why the trip to Sulaco?" he asked with a lift of an eyebrow. "A little rest and relaxation before you got too serious about all this maternal freedom business?" His gaze roamed down her body, indolent and contemptuous, as if he could just imagine how she'd relaxed.

Nikki cringed inside at the galling insult, at the pictures he was forming in his mind. "No," she said, failing to keep the tremor out of her voice. "It was no vacation. Carlos is holding a safe house for the release."

*Carlos.* He'd set himself up for that painful piece of information, Josh thought. But Nikki, beautiful, conniving Nikki . . . He didn't know what kind of game she was setting up. She had a good, straight story, but like the newspaper article, it was too good, too straight, and it was based on an impossible motive: Travinas seeking asylum in the United States. The general would no sooner do that than he'd cut his own throat. Uncle Sam took a very dim view of drug lords, and Travinas had financed his whole revolution through a labyrinthine maze of coca plantations, Caribbean banks, and New Orleans money men.

Either Travinas was using her or she was lying, and he knew the lady too well to believe she would let anybody use her. Every fact and instinct he had told him to walk out the door and never look back.

He'd be damned if he would admit why he was going to stay.

# Seven

Nikki sat on the edge of her bed, a bath towel draped across her shoulders, her head buried in her hands. Many more nights like this and she'd never live to see thirty, she thought. Even a long, stinging hot shower had failed to loosen the tight muscles across the back of her neck. The ache was beginning to rattle her brain.

Outside her door, she could hear Josh prowling through the apartment. For half an hour she'd been listening to him circle through the pair of adobe arches connecting her office and living room. He'd opened the refrigerator three times, undoubtedly for beer, and tried the stereo once.

Sighing, she lifted her head and pushed the skinny strap of her camisole back up on her shoulder. She could have told him the radio only delivered static and rhetoric. Otherwise she would have turned it on hours ago, to fill in the tense silence they'd suffered through until she'd found the grace to show him the guest room and say good night.

Tomorrow would be better. Tomorrow they'd be in

Sulaco, surrounded by Delgado's troops. She'd rest easier when Josh was safe.

But first they had to get there, and for that she needed a helping hand. With another weary sigh, she picked up the phone, pausing in the path to her ear to dial the single digit for the front desk.

When the night clerk answered, she asked him to transfer her to maintenance. When maintenance answered, she asked for Paco.

"Sí?"

"Paco, it's Nikki Kydd. I need ten gallons of gasoline by six o'clock tomorrow morning. Can you get it?"

"Sí. Three dollars a gallon."

She squeezed her eyes shut and rubbed her fingers across her brow. His price was outrageous, but at least he wasn't complaining about short supplies. "A dollar a gallon," she countered.

"Two-fifty."

"Two, and you fill up the tank."

"Deal. Where's your Chevy parked? In front or in back?"

"Two blocks east, on Simeon Boulevard."

A short silence preceded his soft laughter. "You did it to me again, *chica*. Now I have to carry ten gallons of cheap gasoline for two blocks. Just once you should let me make a good deal."

"Next time for sure," she said around a big yawn. "I'll leave your money at the desk." She hung up the phone and again buried her face in her hands. Lord, she hoped she could get some sleep that night.

The apartment dark behind him, Josh stood in front of the French doors, his hands shoved into his pockets, his shoulders square with tension. Nikki had disappeared into her room over an hour ago, but he was still too wound up to go to bed, especially alone.

He carefully scanned the gardens below, north to south and west to east, searching for anything out of place. Nothing about the night felt right. He'd been walking a thin edge since his return, and meeting up with Nikki had only made that edge skinnier, more dangerous. The riots were bad but inconsequential compared to her strange tale of lies. Three years ago she couldn't have lied to him if her life had depended on it.

But three years ago she'd belonged to him, not to some guy named Carlos. Bitterness drew his mouth into a tight line. He'd let her off easy tonight, too easy. He couldn't afford to be that generous in the morning. She had asked him to leave with her for Sulaco at first light and he'd agreed. Not even Nikki wanted to get out of the city more than he did. But he'd have the truth before they set foot outside her apartment. He'd push her as hard as necessary to get it, no holds barred, no backing off because of what was or might have been. The lady had already pushed him to the limit with her lies and her boyfriend.

A flash of movement drew his attention back to the gardens. He instinctively stepped out of sight but kept his eyes trained on the courtyard. Something, or someone, was out there, hiding in the trees. A moment later he knew he'd made the biggest mistake of his life by coming back to Nikki. He turned and ran toward her bedroom, grabbing his satchel on the way.

Nikki woke with a moan, rudely shaken by a hand on her shoulder.

"Get up and get dressed. We're leaving."

"Josh? What?" she mumbled, trying to brush his

hand away and roll back over into her pillows. Even half asleep, she knew whose voice was speaking to her. He was always doing things like that, jostling her awake just because he'd gotten a hot lead. Well, she was too tired to scoop anybody that night. Let somebody else have the front page for a change.

"Move it, Nikki." He peeled the sheet down to the foot of the bed. She started to reach for it, but her hand didn't get as far as her knees before he grabbed her and pulled her up off the pillows. "I said move it."

Nikki struggled, coming awake in rapidly increasing degrees. "What do you think you're doing?" she grumbled, alternately shoving at his hand around her wrist and trying to pull the sheet up over her hips.

"I'm getting the hell out of here, and you're coming with me." He crossed to her closet and jerked the first dark thing he touched off its hanger. "Put this on." He threw the bunched-up garment on the bed.

"Josh, I don't . . . This is my best shirt." She lifted up the simple black silk T-shirt, then shifted her questioning gaze to where he stood demolishing her clothes.

"I'm sure the boys in the garden won't mind if you wear your good shirt. Dammit, Nikki, where are your pants?" He pulled hanger after hanger out of the closet and tossed them to the floor until he found what he wanted.

"Boys?" She caught the fatigue pants that came flying over his shoulder, his urgency starting to light a fire under her even though she had no idea what he was talking about. With the pants pulled up around her waist, she slipped into the silk T-shirt.

"Soldiers. Looks like we're being surrounded. Where are those tennis shoes you were wearing?"

She stopped with her shirt half tucked into her pants. "Josh," she began slowly, watching him dig through the bottom of her closet. "Soldiers on the street at night in San Simeon isn't exactly front-page news these days."

"They're not on the street; they're in the court-yard"—he rounded the end of the bed and stopped barely a foot from her—"and who in the hell is talking about news?" He shoved her tennis shoes into her hands, then reached down and zipped her pants. "Let's go."

"This is crazy," she protested, fighting the awareness sparked by the intimacy of his brief touch.

"I'm leaving."

And he was, with only his satchel strapped across his chest. Nikki hobbled after him, jamming on her shoes. She opened her mouth to explain another line of reasoning, but a sudden pounding on the door halted her in midbreath.

Josh swore softly and vehemently, a single word of disgust. He turned quickly, checking out their limited options. The pounding came again, followed by a commanding voice.

"National Security Force! Open the door!"

Nikki's heart jumped into her throat, racing furiously. *Double-crossed!* But how? Why? Who? The questions flashed across her mind. She whirled and stared at Josh.

"Don't look at me." He picked up her duffel and tossed it to her. "Come on."

She caught the bag and slung the strap over her head and across her chest as she ran after him through the arch to her office. Whatever was going on, she wasn't going to wait there to find out about it, not with the NSF breaking down her door.

He dropped to a crouch in front of the French doors. "I'll go first. You stay behind me and don't do anything stupid." He turned and gave her a lethal glare. "Don't even think it."

The fierce intensity of his threat scared her almost as much as the sounds coming from the hallway. Almost, but not quite. When he eased his body through the door, keeping low and taking care not to rustle the curtains, she followed.

Out on the balcony, the air was a shade cooler, softer, more fragrant. Josh ignored the fire escape on the left, heading straight for the adjacent balcony. Below them, the soldiers appeared and reappeared through the heavy foliage, combing the courtyard. Nikki slipped over the low railing and balanced herself for the three-foot stretch to the next balcony, alternately thanking heaven for the overgrown state of the gardens and cursing the branches and leaves hindering their progress. Vines trailed from the trees to the building, tangling into a morass of shadow. Palms curved their fronds into rustling tendrils against the adobe brick. Josh held her arm for each jump, silently pulling her along behind him.

Four apartments over, they ran out of balconies and came to the last fire escape on the east wing of the Paloma. Going down was out. Up meant a ladder climb to the roof and backing themselves farther into a corner. Josh didn't hesitate in signaling her up, but Nikki had her doubts.

She eyed the rusty ladder, especially the last few unprotected feet at the top. Anybody climbing over the edge of the roof would be in full view of the courtyard for an eternally long moment. She glanced back down into the garden. What had gone wrong? Travinas had nothing to gain and everything to lose by double-crossing her—unless he knew about her deal with Delgado.

Impossible, she thought, but her pulse picked up just the same. If he'd found out, she could forget seeing her next birthday, let alone her thirtieth.

"Whatever you're thinking, it can wait," Josh muttered under his breath. "Get your tail up—" His last word was drowned out by a burst of machine-gun fire.

They both dropped to their knees on the balcony, Nikki with her hands over her head, cringing in the corner, Josh with his body pressed up against hers. But the rain of bullets and chipped brick never came.

"Lord!" Josh exclaimed softly. "They're shooting up your apartment!" He scrambled back to his feet, pulling her with him. "Go!" He pushed her up the ladder and stayed hot behind her all the way to the roof. They fell over the cornice, got up, and started running.

As they ran, Josh singed her ears with a tirade of disjointed cussing and low-level yelling, most of which she was too confused to understand. At the end of the roof, he hauled her to a stop and whipped her around to face him.

"What in the hell is going on?" He ground the words out between clenched teeth, his fingers biting into the tender flesh of her upper arms.

Winded, she gulped for air. "I don't know," she gasped. "You're hurting me."

"I ought to—" He stopped abruptly and jerked his head around.

Nikki heard it, too, the sound of heavy boots rhythmically pounding the pavement, marching down Simeon Boulevard. Her struggles died as a new wave of panic took hold of her heart, pure, undiluted panic. Wild-eyed, she looked up at him.

"Dammit, Nikki," he whispered fiercely. "What have you done?" Fear edged the question, turning anger into desperation.

"Oh, Josh." Her voice caught as his grip tightened. She'd never dreamed it would come to this, whatever this was. "I'm sorry, so sorry."

"Not nearly as sorry as you're going to be," he growled. "Where's your car?" She pointed toward the street and he swore again.

"Two blocks east," she quickly explained.

"Well, that's the first smart thing you've done tonight. Can you jump the alley?"

Her gaze followed his gesture into the dark gap between the buildings, and her mouth dropped open. It was a narrow alley, barely six feet across, a corridor to the street. But the tobacco shop next door was eight feet down.

"That's what I was afraid of." He released her in disgust and clenched his fists. Jerking around, he looked for another way out. When he didn't find one, he turned back to her. "Damn you, Nikki. I'm mad enough to throw you that far. What's it going to be?"

One look at his face confirmed his threat. He'd throw her all right, and none too gently. "I'll jump," she said, swallowing the lump in her throat.

"Good. I recommend a running start."

"Right."

"You first."

"Right." What was she saying?

"We haven't got all night."

"Right." She backed up and took a deep breath.

"Nikki?"

"Yes?"

"Land light on your feet. Bend your knees."

*Right.* Thinking in slow motion and moving in

fast forward, she ran across the roof and lofted herself into space. Josh landed half a minute behind
her, albeit more smoothly than she.

"Are you okay?" he asked, hauling her to her feet.

"Right," she whispered, gasping for breath. She
bent over to ease the stitch in her side, grimacing
with pain.

"You did great."

"Thanks," she muttered. So help her, if she got
out of this alive, she was signing up for a domestic
beat.

He touched her shoulder, letting her know she
had the minute she needed. "We always were a good
team, Nikki. Remember that time at the waterfall?"

"Yes," she said, wary of his detour down memory
lane. She hadn't jumped alone that time, and they
hadn't been running for their lives. They'd been
playing in the water like a couple of kids. He'd scooped
her up in his arms and taken her squealing with
him into the deep pool. It was one of the few times
he'd held her.

She'd been surprised at his strength back then;
everything about him surprised her now—his anger
bordering on surliness at her apartment, the fine-
honed caution that had probably just saved her life,
and the hard look of him, as if life had only gotten
crueler since she'd left him. She refused to think
she was the cause. She didn't have that much confidence in her charms or her hold on him. No other
man had so much as looked at her in three years,
and no man had ever looked at her the way he had
that night. A blush stole up her cheeks, fortunately
hidden by the night. With effort, she straightened
up. "We'd better get going."

"Yeah." He stepped away from her and adjusted
his satchel strap across his shoulder. "We'll go for

the car, if we can get to it. Let's see what we're up against."

Holding her side, she followed him to the front of the tobacco shop where they crouched down behind a large wooden cutout of the proprietor's name. Troops were massed in the street below, replacing the night's rambunctious rioters with a quieter menace.

"I don't get it," Josh whispered.

"What?"

"The whole scene—the blasting of your apartment, the NSF calling in military backup. It's so dramatic, not like their regular game plan of sneaking around, 'disappearing' people. Somebody is trying to make a statement, a big statement. And he's going to be damn mad when he comes up empty-handed, looking like a fool."

Nikki silently agreed. None of this made sense to her. Travinas had a more subtle style, just as deadly, but more discreet. He fancied himself the great manipulator working behind the scene. When things went right, he took all the glory. When things went wrong, somebody else took the heat.

"Who do you think they're after?" Josh asked. "You or me?"

She turned and stared at him, wide-eyed. He'd caught her off guard again. "I—I don't know," she stammered. "Who knows you're here?"

"You."

"Then I guess they're after me." The instant the words were out, she realized she'd made a mistake. So did he.

"And that doesn't make much sense, does it, Nikki? Not with Travinas needing your help."

She opened her mouth to say something, anything, but he cut her off.

"You never were much of a liar, and I'll be damned if I know why you decided to start with me . . . but I'll find out. You can count on it." He let the threat hang between them for a long, tense moment before looking back toward the street.

Any shred of camaraderie they'd built over the last few minutes died with his statement, leaving her feeling more alone than she had in years. He'd done it on purpose, set her up with his fond reminiscing, then gone in for the kill. And she'd been such easy prey. Speechless, she turned away from him, wondering when she'd gotten so stupid, and when he'd gotten so cunning.

"Bingo," he whispered, drawing the word out. "Can you identify the man coming out of the Paloma? The one who looks like somebody starched his shorts?"

Nikki pressed her cheek against the wood sign, peering through the "A" in Sanchez. When she saw the man fitting Josh's description, the fine hairs rose on the back of her neck.

"Is that Brazia?" he asked.

"Yes." Suddenly all the pieces fell into place. Travinas hadn't double-crossed her; his mad dog had tracked Josh down. Tall and thin to the point of emaciation, Brazia skittered down the broad steps fronting the Paloma, barking orders and flailing his arms at the soldiers. "We got to get out of here," she said. "Now."

She turned to leave, but Josh's hand on her arm stopped her. "Just a minute. Who's that?" He pulled her back down and pointed to the street.

Two soldiers were dragging an old man toward Brazia's jeep. Nikki watched in growing horror as they slammed him up against the door. "Paco," she whispered, her arms tightening around her duffel bag.

"Who's Paco?"

"My gasoline connection. He was supposed to fill up my car tonight."

"He knows where your car is?"

"Yes."

Their eyes met, and in the next second they were both running across the roof, racing against time.

# *Eight*

Josh dropped off the roof first, then reached up for Nikki. There was no hesitation this time. She slipped over the edge, her fingers gripping the rain gutter until she felt his hands grab her waist. As soon as her feet touched the ground, he took off down the trash alley, knowing she'd be right behind him all the way. In a year of chasing after stories and running from trouble, he'd only lost her once. The night she'd walked out on him.

Rats fled in front of their flying feet, scurrying under garbage bins and behind trash cans. Rubbish and sewage spilled out of the containers, running a ribbon of stench from the Palacio half a mile west to the river two miles east. On the rare days when the wind came out of the north, Nikki kept her doors closed and burned incense in her apartment, fighting a losing battle with Third World sanitation.

Tonight they only had to get through two blocks of the smell. She did her best to hold her breath, but they were long blocks and the putrid air was gagging her, making her nostrils quiver with revulsion.

At the first cross street, Josh stopped and motioned for her to do the same. A quick check revealed the immediate area to be clear of soldiers, proving that Paco was still holding out.

"How far up are you parked?" he asked, still watching the street.

"The end . . . of the block." She gasped in a lungful of fresher air, her chest heaving. "There's a smaller access alley between the buildings . . . leading to the boulevard. My car's a few yards from it."

Without a word, he grabbed her hand and dashed across the pavement. Nikki clutched her duffel close to her stomach. She was going to be sick. Or she would have been if he'd given her a chance. He didn't, though, and she didn't have the strength either to stop him or to free herself.

Josh knew she was in some kind of distress. Her arm had gone limp in his hand, and she was stumbling along behind him like a rag doll. He cared, but there wasn't a damn thing he could do about it except to keep running and get them out of that hellhole of an alley.

The access corridor wasn't much better, and it was a lot narrower, making every box and can a major hurdle. He dodged the rubble, lashing out with his free arm and his feet to clear a path. Cartons of trash crashed down behind them. He stopped ten feet from the street, and Nikki immediately slumped against the building wall, her eyes shut, her head tilted back.

Ignoring her for another moment, Josh ripped open the zipper on her duffel and rummaged through her stuff until he found her keys. "Stay put," he commanded, shoving the bag back into her hands.

She couldn't have moved if she'd wanted to. She was scared, and something was wrong with her. Her knees were trembling, her stomach churning. Sweat poured down her face and drizzled into a stream between her breasts.

She rubbed her cheek against her shoulder, trying to slow her breathing. Stress, she told herself, too much stress, and that god-awful smell, and Brazia—and Paco. A sob caught in her throat. She'd really done it this time.

In a minute Josh was back at her side, lifting her arm around his shoulder. "We're almost there, Nikki. Help me."

But he didn't need her help. With his other arm around her waist, he lifted her off the ground and half ran to the car. He shoved her inside and slammed the door shut, then vaulted over the hood of the car and slid down the other side. His foot was on the gas pedal, his fingers turning the ignition, even before he had his door closed.

He started the car with a roar, spinning the steering wheel and leaving a U-shaped trail of rubber on Simeon Boulevard. Nikki was doubled over in the seat, one hand braced on the dashboard, the other pressed against her stomach.

Two blocks east a pair of headlights flashed in the rearview mirror. Swearing loudly, Josh made a sharp left turn, throwing her against the door. He grabbed her shoulder and pulled her back to the middle of her seat.

"We've got company."

Nikki groaned in answer.

"How do you feel?"

"I think I'm going to die," she whispered between clenched teeth.

"Not if I can help it," he said grimly, checking the mirror and finding it empty of the two bright spots of light. His hands didn't relax on the wheel, though, and neither did his foot on the accelerator.

The Chevy ate up the miles, skidding around the maze of turns he put it through, taking them deeper into the barrio where the streets were rougher. The small car bounced through the potholes, and Nikki cringed every time the undercarriage hit bottom. The lights of downtown faded to a glow in the night, replaced by the smoking remains of the rioters' bonfires. When they reached the outskirts of the capital, he turned toward the highway, but only got half a block before another car screeched out of a side street onto the main avenue.

"Hold on!" he warned as he slammed on the brakes and swung the wheel in a 180-degree arc. He punched the gas, and the car roared back down the bone-jarring pavement. Nikki's stomach leapt into her throat, lodging in the middle of a knot of nausea and fear. They were going to die. Travinas had covered every escape route. He hadn't given her a chance to pull together her side of their sordid bargain. Or had he found out about Delgado? Had he put her name next to Josh's on Brazia's hit list?

*God save us.* The soundless prayer fell from her trembling lips.

Josh tried to make it to a through street but was cut off again by another car. Not a military vehicle. The odd thought registered, but only for a moment before a jeep came out of nowhere to take up the chase.

Sweat and panic broke out at the same time. He'd never lose all three of them. The ensuing few minutes proved his point. The jeep stayed hot on his tail, but the other two cars were playing cat and mouse with him, falling behind, jumping ahead, shooting through the alleys. One thing he quickly realized was the horsepower advantage they had. He was faster than the jeep, but the two cars were faster than anything he'd seen in San Simeon—and they were confusing the hell out of him. He was about ready to do something crazy, like stop the car and ask them what they were doing, when he got a clue.

During a blur of lights and cars at a crossroad, the jeep took off after the wrong car. He didn't really believe the mix-up had happened on purpose, but neither did he quite believe it was an accident. Thoroughly confused, he tried for the highway again and was cut off by the second car.

He uttered a foul obscenity. They were left with only one way out, the river road. He wheeled the Chevy into the last-chance turn.

"Don't take the river road," Nikki moaned from her huddled position deep in the seat, her head barely above the windowsill. "It dead-ends in about a mile."

"Not quite," he muttered.

True, she knew, but it didn't exactly remain a road, either. She hazarded a quick glance at him. His face was a stony mask, his mouth drawn tight. A small muscle twitched in his jaw, a warning sign she normally would have heeded, but nothing about the night was normal.

"My car doesn't have four-wheel drive," she said, straining to be diplomatic.

He slanted her a hard look and continued driving too fast. The pavement ended abruptly, but that didn't slow him down. If the driver of the other car wanted them, he was going to have to blow a few shocks to get them. Dust billowed up behind and around the Chevy until even the dirt track became lost in an overgrowth of weeds.

Instinct and a faint set of memories guided his hands on the wheel. The trail curved around every giant tree, hearkening back to its history as a footpath from the outlying villages, and it took them deeper into the forest with every turn. Finally, out of necessity, he eased up on the gas pedal.

Shadows and shapes loomed out of the pitch darkness, caught in the gleam of the headlights, but no lights followed them. Josh didn't know whether to be relieved or scared senseless—it was pretty obvious the car driver had allowed him to go this way—so he settled for an intense mix of alertness and unease.

Branches slapped against the car, and the dank odor of mildewing leaves permeated the air. The undergrowth thickened with each mile until he was forced to slow the car to a crawl.

Shaking uncontrollably, Nikki released a heavy breath and pried her fingers off the dashboard. Blindly she groped in the glove compartment, feeling around for the bottle of antacid tablets she'd stashed in there for her Sulaco trip.

Two tablets and five minutes later, she felt the nausea and cramping subside to a manageable level. She would live after all.

Josh heard her sigh and stretch out in the passenger seat, and felt a small measure of his own tension dissipate. A very small measure. She'd pushed him too far this time. He wanted to shake her or hold her or yell at her or something.

"Whatever you took, give me double," he demanded.

She complied by shaking four tablets into his open palm. He popped them into his mouth and immediately grimaced, but he chewed until he got the whole chalky mess down.

"You're a little young to be working on an ulcer, aren't you?"

His accusing tone grated on her already shot nerves. The last thing she needed was a rundown of her shortcomings. "So are you," she countered, not bothering to open her eyes, let alone look at him. Lord! What had happened? She'd had everything under control until he'd shown up, and damn little had gone right since.

"It wasn't me back there holding my gut and shaking like a leaf," he said.

And the last thing she wanted to talk about was her stomach. With luck, she might be able to forget she even had one, an empty, aching one. "This road has changed since the last time we were on it. Nobody uses it anymore. We might not be able to get through to the highway."

"We might not need to."

Her eyes opened to narrow slits. "What's that supposed to mean?"

"It means that unless I get the answers I want, I'm turning this Chevy around and heading back to the city."

Despite the harsh conviction in his voice, she didn't believe him, not for a minute. "I'd heard you'd gotten a little reckless," she said, "but no one mentioned you'd gone crazy."

"Then whoever you were talking to didn't know the whole story," he snapped back, fighting the wheels out of a deep rut. He knew he'd been labeled as one of journalism's "bad boys," but most of the time his reputation worked to his advantage. It kept other reporters out of his stories and kept his editor's expectations high for quality and low for obedience.

"Don't you know who Brazia is?" Her voice rose with doubt, instantly setting him back on the fine edge of anger.

He sat silently fuming, his hands white-knuckling

the steering wheel. Who in the hell was she to question him? He was the one with the questions, and rightly so. He hadn't lied to anybody, and he hadn't traveled a thousand miles to hear her lie to him. Now that he thought about it, he didn't know why in the hell he *had* come back.

He was gearing himself up to tell her just that when the headlights caught a heavy branch lying across the trail. He cut the wheel fast to the right, throwing Nikki over to his side. He slammed his foot down on the brake, and the car lurched to a halt. She thudded into his lap, sprawled over the front seat with one hand digging into his thigh.

"Have you completely lost your mind?" she sputtered, trying to right herself. "Maybe I should—"

He jerked her up, sending her blond hair flying and rattling her teeth. He held her in a viselike grip, her face mere inches from his. "I know Brazia better than his own mother," he said softly, his eyes glittering with menace. "It's *you* I don't know anymore."

Her heart jumped back into her throat. She attempted to move away, back to the safety of her side of the car, but he was having none of it.

His hands tightened painfully on her arms. "It's game time, Nikki, and the game is Twenty Questions. My questions. Your answers."

A strange tremor, very much like fear, coursed down her spine. She squirmed, shaking her shoulders, testing the strength of his grip and finding it unbreakable. Her eyes flashed up to his. "You're scaring me," she said, confessing her fear in the hope it would bring him to his senses. He'd never hurt her before, but he was darn close to doing it now.

"Then we're even," he said. "You've scared me plenty

in the last couple of hours, and I don't take that from anybody."

The sheer arrogance of his remark sparked her anger back to life. "Let go of me, Josh." She squirmed again. "Ask whatever you want, but let go of me."

"Lady," he whispered between his teeth, "I'm not even close to letting go of you."

Before she could protest, he bent his head and took her mouth in a bruising kiss. She gasped and struggled, her awkward position leaving her helpless to break free. He devoured her from the outside in, taking advantage of her parted lips to thrust his tongue inside.

She fought the intrusion, her hands pushing against his chest. Then suddenly he stopped, his mouth still on hers, and with a soft moan he traced her lips, soothing the tender skin with his tongue. The gentle touch and aching sound went through her like heated honey, melting every ounce of sense she had.

"Kiss me, Nikki," he murmured between brushes of his mouth, his breath coming hard. "Kiss me." His arms slid around her in an embrace of pure power, dragging her to her knees and across his chest.

"Don't." She choked out the weak command. "Don't do this to—"

He silenced her with the kiss she didn't want, with the kiss she couldn't stop, teasing her mouth and unraveling her resistance. He caught her lower lip between his teeth, tugged gently, and sent a tumultuous wave of longing through her body.

Coerced by the insistence of his passion and her own weak will, she drew his tongue back into her mouth and died just a little inside. Inevitably, she lost herself in the sensual pleasures he offered—the taste of him, the slow explosions of electricity he created with each touch, the glory of his hard body beneath her, and the safety of his arms around her.

She'd missed him for so long. She'd fought the loneliness and regrets until she'd convinced herself she could live without him, that there would be another man someday.

*Lies, all lies . . .* the truth whispered. Reality faded into a swirling vortex of long-ago emotion and growing excitement. Her hands slipped around his neck as her body slid down his. Josh Rios had been her first man, her only man. He'd been her friend, and one night, one unforgettable summer night, he'd been her lover.

A sweet ache grew between them, needing only a movement here, a touch there, to drown them both. Josh drew her farther on top of him, holding her tighter and closer, his hands cupping her hips, and still he couldn't get enough. He tilted his head and opened his mouth wider over hers, capturing her soft moans and feeling them run like wildfire to his loins. Nikki Kydd still belonged to him, and if she belonged to him, she didn't belong to some guy named Carlos, no matter what she'd said.

Slowly sliding his hands up to her face, he lifted his mouth from hers and looked into her languid, passion-smudged eyes. His thumbs caressed the delicate angle of her jaw. "You've got a lot to learn, Nikki," he said huskily. "And the first lesson is don't lie to me. Who is Carlos?"

She stared at him in confusion, her chest hurting with the effort to breathe, her arms heavy with the need to hold him again.

The longer she looked at him, at his dark angel face and the faint sheen of dampness on his skin, the more aware she became of where she was, of what she'd done. A heated blush stole up her cheeks. She was all over him, straddling his hips, her hands on his shoulders, her fingers tangled in his hair—and she'd kissed him with passion, exposing herself in the most vulnerable way possible.

"Damn you," she whispered, trying not to die of shame and embarrassment. She quickly scrambled back to her side of the seat, and this time he let her go.

"You've already done a good job of that, Nikki." His voice carried across the darkness without a trace of the tenderness he'd just shown. "Now answer my question."

"No," she said, shaking inside. "Do what you have to, Josh. But I'm not playing your game tonight, any of your games." It was a calculated risk, an emotionally calculated one, but he was manipulating her too easily for her to engage in a battle of wits, let alone a battle of kisses and memories. Exhaustion and stress had lengthened the odds against her. She wasn't thinking fast enough to win, and win she must, at any cost.

Two days, she prayed, wrapping her arms around her waist and shivering despite the thick, heavy heat pressing all around her. Just let her have two days without making any more mistakes. Two days to set everyone up. Two days before he realized what she'd done.

Two days without making a complete fool of herself, she added with a stifled groan, slipping farther down in the seat and closing her eyes. Even at a hundred percent, she wouldn't be a match for his mind-weakening style of sensual persuasion.

Josh watched her shut herself away from him, and he knew he'd blown it, in spades. He hadn't meant to kiss her. He hadn't meant to get side-tracked on her personal life, which he admitted hadn't gotten him very far. But then, she'd never been easy to push around.

Some things never changed, he thought, tightening his hands around the steering wheel and dropping his head back in frustration. Not her stubbornness, not her exasperating ability to pull him in over his head, and not his reaction to her touch. His body still pulsed with arousal, a deep throbbing he had only himself to blame for. She hadn't teased him; he'd plunged in with his heart and soul bared.

Once, they'd gotten love right, so perfect that every other woman he'd had left him feeling empty—but not nearly as empty as he felt now.

With a resigned sound from deep in his throat, he sat up and eased the car forward, taking care not to hit the tree branch lying across the dirt track.

Nikki woke to a pale, hazy dawn filled with soft shadows and light, and the chattering of birds. Mist drifted down from the canopy of trees. The leaves of the lower plants glistened with a misleading dewy freshness. Nothing was fresh in this tropical forest sauna.

She rolled to a sitting position in the seat, unconsciously reaching up and kneading the sore muscles in her neck and shoulders. A hundred yards ahead, the road opened up and the forest thinned out, giving way to savanna. She noted the fact, then glanced in the backseat.

He was crammed into the small space, one knee bent, the other leg stretched under the front seat. His chest rose and fell softly. His hair was damp and slicked back from his face, heavy with the humidity and sweat that also moistened his face and his clothes. A night's growth of beard stubbled his jaw.

As she watched him, he shifted uncomfortably, rearranging his shoulders and hips. He grimaced at the futile effort and fell back into his original position. Compassion told her to wake him, to put him out of his misery. Common sense told her he needed all the rest he could get, no matter how uncomfortable. She certainly felt better after her sleep, more in control, less susceptible to the previous night's volatile mix of tension, fear, and spontaneous combustion.

Combustion. There was no other word for what had happened to her when he'd kissed her. She'd lost all reason under the pliant assault of his mouth, under each caress of his hands. She sighed and dragged her fingers through her hair, her gaze drifting beyond the windshield. Forget it, Nikki, she told herself. Forget it and save yourself a whole lot of heartache.

Behind her, Josh opened his eyes, and the first thing he saw was the woman who had run him ragged in his dreams. He felt like hell, and she looked gorgeous, a recently acquired talent, he guessed. She never used to look that good first thing in the morning. He remembered a gawky girl with a cap of tousled hair, her eyes bloodshot from too many beers the night before, her mood grumpy for the same reason. He hadn't made much of a guardian.

When he'd finally become aware of her miraculously transforming body and his own reaction to the change, he'd made damn sure he didn't see her first thing in the morning anymore. The overnight camp-outs had come to a halt, and so had the shared hotel rooms. The cost of an extra room had been a small price to pay for his sanity.

He'd lost it anyway, and what had it gotten him?

Months of desperation, years of trying to forget, and all so he could end up in the middle of nowhere in the backseat of a Chevy, alone. The gods must be laughing.

"Good morning," he lied.

"Good morning." Her eyes met his briefly before she turned away. "Where are we?"

"We're where the gas ran out." She did look beautiful. Her hair was tousled, but it didn't used to tousle into a golden mane. Her eyes weren't bloodshot. They were clear, and still the palest summery green he'd ever seen. Her mood was a mystery, but not for long.

"I told you not to take this road."

Damn, he thought. The lady had a diagram of all of his buttons, and she was determined to keep pushing the one marked "mad."

"You told me a lot of things last night," he said, "and I didn't believe any of them." He pushed himself up and reached for his satchel, trying not to notice how the silky T-shirt clung to her breasts and fell off one shoulder, or how the skinny black strap of her slip looked against her creamy skin.

She had great shoulders. No amount of satchel-rummaging could distract him from that particular fact. Finally he found what he wanted.

Nikki watched him unscrew the lid of a metal flask and raise the container to his mouth.

"What have you got?" she asked.

In answer, he handed her the flask and continued swishing the liquid around in his mouth. She took a small sip, and her eyes widened.

"Whiskey," he rasped.

"*Cheap* whiskey," she corrected him. She inhaled deeply and felt her sinuses clear all the way to the tips of her toes. Immediately her stomach told her it didn't appreciate the crude addition.

She popped two of the antacid tablets into her mouth, for the first time wondering if maybe she *was* working on an ulcer.

"Sorry. I forgot," he said.

"Don't worry about it. Do you want something to eat?"

He leaned forward and looked out the windshield, both eyebrows lifted. "Do you see something I don't? Like a restaurant? Or a bunch of bananas?"

"No. I've still got my Sulaco provisions in the trunk. Nothing fancy, but it'll keep us from starving until we figure out what we're going to do."

"Walk," he said.

"What?"

"We're going to walk. There's a ranch about a mile up the road."

She tilted her head and gave him a quizzical look. "How do you know that?" She lived in San Simeon, and she hadn't known where this branch of the river road led to.

"A year ago I was in and out of here quite a bit."

Try as she might, she couldn't keep the disappointment and the hurt off her face. He'd been in San Simeon a number of times and he hadn't contacted her. Any illusions she'd had about their friendship died with the knowledge.

"I stopped looking for you a long time ago, Nikki," he said softly, hating himself for putting the bleakness in her eyes, and hating her for allowing him the power to hurt her. What he knew but didn't say was that it had taken everything he had not to go looking for her again. Every time his plane had touched down in San Simeon, he'd fought the same useless battle.

She nodded and hurried out of the car before she did something stupid, like cry.

Josh lowered his head and shook it from side to side, swearing under his breath. What had she expected him to do? She was the one who had left him, left him to wake up alone. If anyone ever asked him what was the worst day of his life, he would have a few to choose from, but only one true contender.

Even before he'd fully awakened that morning, he'd been dreaming about making love to her again, his Nikki, his woman. He knew there had been a smile on his face, kind of a crazy smile, full of amazement and a deep, overwhelming satisfaction. He'd wanted to reexplore the wonders of sex with someone he loved. He'd wanted to look into her eyes and discover with her the new meaning they had for each other. An hour later he'd stormed out of the Casa del Flores, leaving a busted-up hotel room and his last dollar behind him.

He'd hoped never to be that angry again, that full of rage and confusion. She'd pushed him damn close the night before—and yet he still felt guilty for hurting her.

Nikki made a whole theatrical arrangement out of ignoring him when he came to stand beside her in front of the open trunk.

"Looks good," he said.

She shrugged and closed her pocket knife against her thigh. "Will two be enough?" she asked, gesturing to the makeshift tortilla and cheese sandwiches rolled up on the cooler.

"Plenty. Do you have anything to wash them down with?"

"Apple juice and beer."

"Juice. For you too."

She slanted him a wry glance. He returned it in full measure.

"I don't want to have to carry you all the way to

the ranch," he explained, and took a big bite out of one of the sandwiches. "How much money do you have?"

"Five hundred colons and fifty American."

"And I've got about two hundred American. Looks like financially we're in pretty good shape."

She wanted to ask "for what?" but she didn't dare rock the boat. So far, he was still heading forward, toward Sulaco, and she didn't want to do or say anything that might make him question his actions.

# *Nine*

"When we get there, let me do all the talking."

"Well, that ought to be a real good trick," she drawled, doubting if he'd get very far with a Spanish vocabulary of "beer," and "where's the bathroom." The tender places of her heart still stung from his earlier admission, though she preferred to think it was only her pride involved. She'd gone through hell leaving him, and he'd never looked back except in anger. Damn him. And damn her for having been so young and foolish, so easy. Her hand stiffened on the strap of her duffel bag.

Josh ignored her sarcasm and kept walking. She matched him stride for stride across the flat fields of thigh-high grass. When they passed the first set of outbuildings belonging to the ranch, a large rambling house came into view. The white walls gleamed in the morning sun. The timbered roof stretched out over the wide front porch running the full length of the house.

Her first glimpse of the building triggered a wave of unease. When Josh had said "ranch," she'd expected the usual two-bit cattle operation, not this palatial spread. From its well-kept appearance to the new truck parked in the driveway, the place had an aura of power and of confidence in the future. Anybody flourishing under Travinas's dictatorship was unlikely to be friendly toward a couple of foreign reporters, especially her. Though she filed her stories without bias, she'd never made a secret of her political leanings.

"I don't think this is a good idea," she said, her steps faltering.

"Do you have a better one?"

"No, but—"

"Then let me do the talking," he repeated as a man came out of the house carrying a rifle, a standard piece of equipment in San Simeon for anyone who could afford one. Another man walked toward them from the barn.

Nikki's gaze darted between the two men. She didn't recognize either of them, so she decided to give Josh a chance, but only a small one. The instant he stumbled, she was going to take over. She figured it would take him about thirty seconds to run through his repertoire and out of conversation.

Josh didn't miss her warning glance, and he found her lack of confidence in him astounding, especially after the previous night. What did she think he'd been doing all these years? Writing a gossip column?

Working hard to keep the anger off his face, he raised a hand in greeting and formally introduced himself as Juan Alonso. Then he proceeded to tell a tale of a camping trip gone bad, of a miscalculation of their gasoline supply, of entomological specimens he had to get back to his camp in La Rosa.

And for every word that fell from his lips in perfect Spanish, Nikki's mouth dropped open another degree. She stared at him until she realized what she was doing.

Dumbfounded, she forced her attention back to the man standing on the porch. Up close, she noticed he was taller than most of his countrymen. Gray streaked his coal black hair at the temples. His shoulders were broad, his white shirt and khaki slacks expensive and tailored to perfection. His stern visage had softened, but he was looking at her, not Josh.

"Señorita Kydd?" he asked with the slightest of questions, the barest hint of a smile, and all of her misgivings returned in full force. It was too late to disappear back into the forest, and there was no advantage in denying the truth. He'd know she was lying, and he'd wonder why.

"Yes," she replied, keeping her distance and wondering what the odds were on outrunning a rifle shot.

"Luis. Luis Cardena." His smile broadened, and he waved the ranch hand over before returning his attention to her. "We met at the Paloma Grand during the Agricultural Summit. You were part of the hounding press, and I was one of the beleaguered proponents of conservation."

"Of course," she said politely, still not quite placing him. But as she recalled, the beleaguered men at the summit had been bucking the system. They weren't a part of it. She gave him her best business smile and wished San Simeon weren't so damn small.

As if sensing her confusion, he added helpfully, "We were supposed to have dinner together the night the rebels took Sulaco." His glance switched to Josh, and his eyes narrowed thoughtfully, curiously. "That's not too far from La Rosa. Only a few miles. You must have heard the fighting."

Josh nodded, but gave no further acknowledgment. He was too busy condemning himself for not listening to her objections. Because of her age, her gender, and her mother, Nikki did have a higher profile than most journalists, but he'd thought she'd be unknown in the countryside. Worse yet, Cardena not only knew her, he'd had a date with her. A date! And from the looks of her, she didn't remember a thing about it. What kind of life was she leading anyway?

"Oh, yes," she said to Cardena, her smile softening before his very eyes. "I'm sorry I ran out on you at the last minute, but in this business, war always takes precedence over agriculture. If I'd known the rebels had planned a major offensive that night, I wouldn't have made any of the summit."

"And if I'd known beforehand how lovely you are, I would have asked them to delay the mission for a few more hours." His gaze drifted down her slender body and slowly came back up to her eyes. "Maybe another night?"

"I'm—"

"Married," Josh interjected, reaching the end of his tolerance for this particular game. He didn't give a damn if she flirted on her own time, but she was on his clock until he decided otherwise.

Without missing a beat, she slipped her arm through his. "We're on our honeymoon," she said, slanting an adoring look up at him from under her gold-tipped lashes.

For an instant, just an instant, Josh believed what he saw in her eyes, and it wrecked a considerable amount of havoc on his unruly mood. But the moment passed, and he accepted the look for what it was, a silent agreement to do things his way for a while. He was gratified and surprised, and more than a little wary.

"Then congratulations are in order. You are a very lucky man, Señor . . . Alonso." Cardena spoke the name slowly, and Josh wondered if he imagined the shade of skepticism.

Plastering a false smile to his face, he said, "I'd feel a whole lot luckier if we could buy a few gallons of gas from you."

"Without question. My gasoline is your gasoline." Cardena laughed at the turned phrase. With effort, Josh worked up a corresponding chuckle.

Nikki was glad they were both having such a good time. So glad, in fact, she wanted to give Josh a good kick. Hadn't he heard the man? Didn't he know when a story fell out of the blue? Luis Cardena had all but confessed to being involved with the rebels, and she was itching to find out more, like which faction. Was he involved with Delgado? Did he know what was happening in Sulaco?

She'd left Sulaco only the previous morning, but in the volatile world of San Simeon politics, the mantle of power switched hands faster than a juggler flipped bowling pins.

"We'll need to borrow a gas can," Josh said, interrupting another appreciative visual survey of Nikki by Cardena.

"Of course," Cardena said, dragging his gaze away from her and turning toward the ranch hand. "Armando, fill up one of our gasoline cans for the señor." He directed his attention back to Josh. "Why don't we settle the señora inside? My housekeeper could make us some breakfast, if you like."

Josh opened his mouth to refuse, but Nikki beat him to the punch. "That would be wonderful," she said, mounting the steps to the porch.

As she followed Cardena inside, she searched her mental files for any tidbit of information she might have come across about him. San Simeon's elite was made up of a very small circle of rich and influential men, and she'd been around long enough to have met them all more than once. Except Luis Cardena. Wealthy landowners usually fell into one category— friends of General Travinas—but Cardena had already shaken her conviction on that point. If he was a holdover from the old days when the rich had been a privileged class for which birth was the only entrée, then he was walking as thin a line as she and Josh, maybe thinner.

Lord, she'd be glad to get out of San Simeon, out of the whole of Central America. She'd had enough political intrigue to last her a lifetime and, after last night, enough of danger to last her two.

Josh entertained similar thoughts as Cardena led them through a wide quarry-tiled hallway to a patio on the north side of the house. He was sick and tired of not knowing what was going to happen next, like this impromptu tête-à-tête. He started to ask himself what in the world Nikki had been thinking, but he didn't bother to complete the question. He didn't have any idea what she'd been thinking.

It wasn't the first time.

The patio Cardena led them to was a botanical delight, a cool expanse of tile and latticework dripping with lush greenery and tropical blooms. He gestured toward a round table in the center. "I've been following your career quite closely over the last year, señora. You seem to have a remarkable knack for the 'scoop.' "

"Call me Nikki, please," she said, settling into a chair. "I guess I have been luckier than some."

"I doubt if luck has anything to do with it . . . Nikki."

Josh cast his eyes heavenward. That was all he needed, an hour listening to this guy gush over her.

"Especially last week," Cardena continued. "A rare coup, indeed, reading the general's mind. Many of us would pay dearly for such a talent."

The words, though casually spoken, rang an instant warning in her mind. She shifted uncomfortably in her chair. Josh leaned forward in his. This was getting interesting.

"It's a matter of sources more than talent," she said, trying to add a breezy note to her voice. But Cardena wasn't put off that easily.

"Then the talent must be in finding the right sources. Yours must be very well connected."

"I've been working this beat for a long time." Somehow she got the feeling Cardena knew exactly how well connected her source had been on the story she'd filed for Josh's sake. She wished he'd quit talking about it. The curious gleam in Josh's eyes hadn't gone unnoticed, and that particular gleam always meant trouble.

With a nod, Cardena rose from the table. "If you'll excuse me, I'll see if I can find Elena."

Nikki waited until he'd disappeared. Then she opened with the most innocuous statement she could dream up. "Nice place."

"Real nice," Josh agreed. "Do you want to tell me what we're doing here?"

"We ran out of gas on the wrong road," she said, letting her gaze travel over the plants, the rattan furniture, the mosaics in the floor. Anywhere except into the steel blue eyes she felt boring into her.

"Good try . . . but try again."

"You're the one who suggested coming here." She shrugged, as if it were a matter of little concern.

"But you're the one who decided to move in. Why?"

Had he always been this persistent? she wondered, almost but not quite regretting her hasty decision. Cardena's personal comments had thrown her off balance, but she still wanted to pump him for information.

"Curiosity?" Josh prompted.

"Yes," she finally admitted, bringing her gaze back to him. "I'm curious about Luis Cardena, about his involvement with the rebels."

"Better, but I'm not buying. Half the country is involved with the rebels. They're not exactly a secret organization," he said dryly.

"True, but I've never heard of him before."

He let her words sink in, settle down, and simmer to a slow boil. "Well, that's a helluva confession, Nikki. Do you make a habit of having dinner with strangers?"

"As a matter of fact, yes," she shot back, bridling under his insinuation. "Usually two or three times a month. In this business I think that's under par for the course." Didn't she have enough to worry about without him bucking her at every turn?

"I don't think *business* is what he had in mind." His voice rose dangerously. "Unless it was *funny business.*"

Her hand only got halfway to his face before he caught it, his palm slapping against her wrist, his fingers tightening and holding her arm in the air.

Shocked by her reaction as much as his furious words, Nikki stared at him, her chest and throat tight with anger. "Don't you dare question my ethics," she choked out, "or my morals."

"Or your actions or that line of bull you fed me

last night or why you left me at the Casa del Flores."
He punctuated each forbidden topic with a corresponding tug on her wrist, pulling her closer. Then
suddenly he released her arm and fell back into his
chair, looking totally disgusted.

Nikki sat in silence, rubbing her bruised wrist
and forcing herself to count to ten. One word, one
wrong word, and they'd be at each other's throats.
At this point she didn't need or want an all-out war
with him. What she needed was to get him to Sulaco
in one piece.

With that in mind, and keeping a firm rein on her
tongue, she apologized. Sort of. "I'm sorry you misunderstood about the dinner." Her lips barely moved.

"I'm sorry I misunderstood a lot of things," he
said, not sounding the least bit apologetic.

Not to be dissuaded, she continued. "The dinner
was a group affair. They wanted some favorable press,
and since I am one of the better-known journalists
in this country, they were hoping to get it from me.
I'm sure you've been wined and dined by people
wanting a favorable slant on their pet project."

Her look said, "Don't you dare tell me you haven't
been," but he could have said no without a twinge of
conscience. The kind of people he'd been investigating never dealt with the press, except at the wrong
end of a gun. Even as a potential customer, he'd
never been wined and dined. Offered a freebie high,
yes. Wined and dined, no.

But he wasn't ready to tell her about Travinas, not
yet, not until he knew what she'd gotten him into
last night, and what she'd gotten him into less than
ten minutes ago.

"What makes you think Cardena is involved with
the rebels?"

Nikki accepted the question as a tentative olive

branch, considering it the least dangerous topic of conversation available. "You heard what he said outside, about asking them to delay the Sulaco mission."

"I don't think he meant it literally, and I can't believe you did either. The man made it clear what he was after."

She looked away. He sounded more bored than angry, and for some ridiculous reason that hurt almost as much as his previous slur on her character.

"And I think you're wrong. Anybody with his kind of money in this country is into either drugs or politics—"

"Or both," he interrupted.

"Or both. But with Cardena, I think it's politics."

"That's generous of you, but a mite naive." In his experience, just about everyone with power south of the Rio Grande was into drugs, directly or indirectly, and the farther south a person went, the worse it got. San Simeon was pretty far south.

"Do you know something I don't?" she asked.

"Not about Cardena."

"Then let's go with my gut feeling and try to find out if he knows what's happening in Sulaco."

"Let's not."

And had he always been this stubborn? "Why?"

"For starters, I told him we were going to La Rosa, and if you don't mind, I'd rather not be exposed as a liar, as a journalist, or as Joshua Rios. So let's go with *my* gut feeling and skip breakfast."

"We've already accepted."

"You accepted," he corrected her. "Change your mind. You're good at that."

"Now what in the hell is *that* supposed to mean?" She threw her hands up in the air in frustration. "Lord, Josh! Did we always fight like this?"

"Yes," he said curtly.

"Then how did we ever get the stories out?" she asked, truly perplexed.

"Desperation," he replied, a grin twisting his mouth. "It was either work or starve."

Despite her best intentions, Nikki felt an answering smile touch her lips. "Well, it doesn't get much more desperate than this. Can we call a truce?"

"Only if you let this story go and leave with me now." Neither his tone nor his countenance left any room for compromise.

"Okay," she said, recognizing a total defeat when she suffered one. If he had known all the reasons she wanted to question Luis Cardena, she might have persuaded him to stay. But compared to the advantage of possible updated information on Delgado, the risk of alienating Josh was too great. Besides, she thought, she'd manipulated him into being anxious to get to Sulaco. Never one to look a gift horse in the mouth, she pushed away from the table.

Silently, he rose with her, and together they made their way back through the wide hallway. Cardena's voice coming from one of the side rooms brought them both to a halt. Nikki started to make their presence known, but Josh's hand on her shoulder stopped her.

"Yes," Cardena said into the telephone, his back to the door. "I have both of them here. I'm sure it's him. He gave his name as Juan Alonso, but he fits the description, and they seem very close. . . . No, my friend, it was not luck. Your men did their job last night. There are only two tracks out of the river road. They were bound to run into me or the men I stationed at the other outlet."

Josh had heard enough, more than enough. They *had* been herded like sheep to the slaughter last night. The realization galled him to the core. Sliding his hand down her arm, he urged her to go forward, but she balked. His eyes widened meaningfully. Now was not the time for indecision, bickering, or hanging around.

*Gas*, she mouthed, adding emphasis by lifting her eyebrows.

Well, he was damn sorry they didn't have any gas, but the tightening of his fingers told her he didn't think this was the place to get it.

But Nikki knew they wouldn't get very far without it, and she for one was willing to play Cardena along for a while to get it.

Josh wasn't. He pushed her forward with a force that brooked no argument.

Softly and quickly, they slipped down the hall to the front door, Josh propelling her all the way. He'd rather take their chances on foot in the forest than sit around waiting for Cardena and his friend to make their decisions for them.

The creak of bootsteps on the wooden porch sounded through the screen door, and Josh pulled her to a stop. He slid his hand inside his satchel and pulled out a gun. Nikki's heart plummeted.

Josh sneaked up to the door and peered around the jamb. When he caught a glimpse of the ranch hand descending the steps, he felt the first glimmer of hope he'd had since he'd jumped back into Nikki's life and landed in a pile of trouble. Armando had left the gas can sitting on the porch. Josh waited a few more seconds, counting the other man's strides away from the house. When he figured it was as safe as it was going to get, he opened the door and whispered, "Run."

Nikki bolted across the porch, heading straight for the forest. Josh grabbed the gas can and ran up the driveway, pocketing the gun and pulling out a knife. He ducked behind the far side of the pickup truck and slashed two of the tires, buying them precious time. Then he lit out behind her, legs pumping, the gas can bouncing against his thighs and straining the muscles in his arms.

Grunting with exertion, he caught up with her at the last ranch building. His instinct was to reach out and take her arm, but he knew she'd be faster on her own.

*"Alto!"* The cry to stop came from behind them, followed by the slamming of a door and a gunshot.

Cardena missed. Josh swore. "Pick it up, Nikki!"

She was already flying, her feet flattening tufts of grass, her arms working like pistons. But at his command, and with the powerful incentive of the rifle's report ringing in her ears, she found an extra burst of speed. She passed him in a blur of khaki legs and streaming blond hair.

Josh let her hold the lead and would have given a year's wages for any kind of break in the austerely flat landscape, a hill, a ditch, anything they could drop out of sight behind or in. He heard the truck engine fire up.

A grim smile flickered across his mouth. He focused his concentration on the line of trees ahead and tried not to remember how long it had been since he'd run a mile. His chest hurt. His muscles burned. The gas sloshed back and forth in the can, threatening to throw him off balance with every footfall.

*I can make it. . . . I can make it.* The litany ran ceaselessly in Nikki's mind, convincing her long past the time when her legs and lungs told her to throw in the towel. Huffing and puffing, a stitch in her side, she jogged the last few yards into the forest and collapsed against a tree.

Josh kept going, afraid to lose the momentum he'd gained. Within the protective shadows of the forest, she'd be safe until he got the car started. Then what? According to Cardena there was a welcoming party waiting for them at the end of the other road out of there, wherever that was. They must have passed the junction in the dark. Not that it mattered. He wasn't going back for anybody or anything. They'd have to take their chances crossing the ranch again.

Great, he thought, thoroughly disgusted with the whole situation and with himself for letting her drag him into it. If they got out of this alive, he was going to . . . going to . . . Hell, he didn't know what he was going to do, but he could guarantee she wasn't going to like it.

He dropped the can at the rear of the car and fell gasping over the trunk, his fingers twisting the gas cap off. She wasn't going to like anything from there on out, because this was his show now. He'd had enough of mystery, of men with guns, of running his guts out. The gas glugged into the empty tank. When the last drop fell, he tossed the can into the trees and stumbled into the car.

Nikki heard him coming, fast and furious down the rutted track, driving her little Chevy as if it were a tank. She pushed off the tree, keeping one arm wrapped around her waist. He lurched to a stop, barely giving her time to get in before he took off again. The forward motion of the car whipped the door closed behind her.

Biting her lip against the pain and not caring what he thought, she flipped the glove compartment open and grabbed the bottle of antacid tablets. When she had three in her mouth, she slumped back against the seat and silently prayed for relief.

Josh glanced at her out of the corner of his eye. She looked awful. Sweat beaded her brow and ran into her hair, turning the golden strands dark. Her skin was pale, her facial muscles tight.

"Buckle up," he ordered, getting angrier with each passing second. Dammit, she should take better care of herself.

With hands made weak by a trembling nausea, she did as she was told, wrapping the safety belt across her shoulder and waist.

The car bounced and flew down the dusty track. True to its name, the road followed the river, skirting the far reaches of the ranch. Up by the house, Josh saw Cardena and Armando double-timing the tire changes, but he knew they couldn't work fast enough to catch him and Nikki. Not the way he was driving—heedless of every rut, skimming the obstacles, sliding through the curves—like a man with nothing left to lose but his life.

# Ten

"Where are we now?" Josh asked.

Biting back a smart remark, Nikki checked the creased and folded map in her hands, then looked out the window at the landscape slipping into shadows drawn by the setting sun. The savanna was long behind them, replaced by the forested mountains of northern San Simeon.

"About ten or fifteen miles from Sulaco," she replied, forcing a helpful tone into her voice.

Josh glanced at the gas gauge. "We're not going to make it."

She pressed her lips tighter together. If he expected her to be surprised, he was in for a rude awakening. Any fool could have figured out his bit of news. Hell, she'd known it for at least the last half-hour.

They'd bartered for fuel at one of the small villages they'd passed earlier in the day, but in a country made up of wandering back roads and meandering byways, a tank of gas didn't go very far. Especially if someone insisted on wandering and meandering along those self-same byways.

"We should have taken the highway," she muttered under her breath, unable to hold her frustration in any longer. For emphasis, she snapped the map with a loud crack.

Josh's jaw went tight. "Let's not get into it again . . . please."

Their truce had gone down in flames the first time he'd ignored her directions. She didn't know what he was up to, but she knew he had something up his sleeve. He'd been too quiet for too long. Not once had he asked her for anything other than directions he didn't bother to follow. She should have been grateful. Instead she was sinking into surliness under the weight of his silent treatment.

"Now where are you going?" she asked in exasperation as he turned onto a road even worse than the one they were on.

Josh checked the sun, his watch, the gas gauge, and decided to tell her the truth. "North."

"North?"

He nodded and raked a hand through his hair, sweeping it back behind his ear and over his collar. He looked beat, she thought. A fine layer of dust dulled the stripes in his shirt and clung to the hairs on his forearms. Faint smudges of weariness darkened the skin below his eyes. Nikki felt awful knowing she was the cause, but she wasn't about to tell him so.

"There's a lot of north up ahead. Could you be a little more specific?"

He shot her a quick look. "The border."

"The border?" Her brow furrowed with a bad premonition. "We don't have to go all the way to the border. Sulaco is five miles in."

His continued silence confirmed the worst. He had no intention of going to Sulaco, hadn't had any such intention since they'd left the ranch. No wonder they'd been switchbacking the countryside like a mule with a burr under its tail.

"You're making a big mistake," she said, quelling a burst of panic and reaching for her antacids. "A big mistake. We have to go to Sulaco." Brazia wouldn't care what side of the border they were on if he caught up with them. And Josh, she knew, wouldn't go quietly. She popped two of the tablets into her mouth and ground them to a paste.

"No, Nikki. You're the one who made a mistake. If you want to tell me about it, maybe"—he cocked a brow in her direction—"maybe we can work out a compromise to get you back to your boyfriend." The lie slipped out smoothly, devoid of his instinctive urge toward sarcasm. He'd decided what he was going to do with her, and nothing was going to stop him. Once before he'd tried to get her out of the country and failed. He wasn't about to fail this time, not when everyone in San Simeon seemed to want a piece of her.

But neither did he want to delve too deeply into his reasons. He might concede a quirk of masculine pride. He refused to acknowledge the possibility of love. The last twenty-four hours had beaten that stupid notion out of him. No sane man would love a woman who put him through what Nikki was putting him through—a wringer of danger and deceit.

Still, when he looked at her, nervous and overwrought, chewing those damn tablets as if her life depended on them, he knew he cared. And when she kissed him, he still wanted her with a fierce possessiveness he'd never felt for any other woman.

Certifiable, he thought, letting out a heavy breath.

They were on the verge of getting lost again—Nikki tasted it in the air, felt it in her bones—and this time they would run out of gas for good. She kept well to her side of the seat and tried to figure out what to do when the Chevy gasped its last drop of petrol. She made a point of ignoring his offer of compromise. Her plan, however messed up it had gotten, had no room in it for compromise. Arriving in Sulaco alone would get her nothing, not her mother's freedom, not Josh's safety, nothing.

"That's it," he announced as he steered the car to a stop under the tangled branches of an overgrown tree. Dirt and gravel crunched beneath the tires with ever-lessening sound until the dusk's silence fell completely about them.

They sat listening to each other breathe, Josh with his hands on the steering wheel, his arms straight and stiff, his shoulders up around his ears, Nikki with her fists clamped around the map, both of them staring out the windshield.

One way or the other, whatever it took, she had to get him to Sulaco.

And he was taking her to the border if he had to hog-tie her and drag her there.

"We—"

"You—"

They had both spoken at once, not much, just a single word apiece, but enough to cause her to reconsider her hastily formed demand. She wasn't in a position to demand anything of him. She'd have to think, use her head and probably part of the truth to get him to Sulaco.

"We can't stay here," she said, gathering up her stuff. Any step forward was still a step in the right direction until they passed Sulaco, which she was determined not to do. She'd think of something. She always thought of something.

"Don't forget your Life Savers." He lifted his hips and shoved the car keys into his back pocket. Then he reached behind them for his satchel.

His arm brushed her shoulder. Their eyes met for an instant before she quickly glanced away, chiding herself for foolishness and an oversensitivity to his touch. She leaned forward an unnecessary degree to retrieve her antacid tablets from the glove compartment.

Josh swore silently and dragged the satchel into his lap. She didn't have to worry about him touching her. He'd learned his lesson the night before. Every time he touched her crazy things happened, things they didn't finish, and things he couldn't forget. No, he was better off keeping his hands and his foolish thoughts to himself.

Little was said as they transferred supplies from the trunk to his satchel and her duffel bag. They'd prepared for a hundred camping trips in much the same manner. Nikki took the food and the sleeping bag, and Josh took the bottles of juice and beer, and a poncho to use as a ground sheet. Neither commented on the lack of a second sleeping bag. They'd make do. They always had before without any problems. Of course, that had been when they were both more wrapped up in any story they were investigating than in each other.

The forest began to thicken twenty feet off the road and continued to thicken until Nikki thought somebody should mention the fact.

"I think we should stick with the road." She slapped back at a leaf slapping her.

"I don't."

Okay, she thought, and tried another tack. "It will take us days to get through this stuff."

"One night and one day," he corrected her.

A twig caught in her hair, jerking her to a stop. She swore and snapped it off, leaving a piece tangled around a few sweaty strands of hair. "You've got all the answers, haven't you," she muttered.

He whirled around so fast, she bumped into him. "No, Nikki! You're the one with all the answers, and until you give them to me, we're doing things my way!" he shouted and jabbed the air with his finger. "So either start talking or save your energy for walking!"

She stumbled back a step, startled by his tirade. He dragged a hand through his hair, shaking his head and swearing through closed teeth. Then he turned on his heel and crashed forward, breaking tree limbs and stomping foliage into the mud.

Nikki watched him, catching her breath and nervously wiping the back of her hand across her mouth. She was going to have to tell him the truth, and soon. One more lie, one more evasion, and he'd walk right out of her life.

The sun hung in the sky, holding back the night and any chance she had of dropping with exhaustion. They'd been trudging through the tangle of undergrowth for only an hour, but little sleep, less food, and a heavy burden of guilt were taking a toll on her waning reserves of energy. Following his advice, she wasted none of it on talking.

She crawled the last few yards up a crumbling limestone shelf to the top of a hill. Josh lay flat on his stomach, perusing the landscape through his binoculars.

"Glad you could make it."

"I bet," she gasped, dropping to her knees beside him. Either he'd burned off his anger with the strenuous hike or it had been sweated out of him by the same heavy, wet heat drenching her skin and making her head pound. She pressed her hands against her thighs, her fingers clenched, her chest rising and falling with shallow breaths.

Even without the binoculars, she could see the village of Sulaco, nestled into a curve of the valley bisected by the river. Makeshift barracks spread across part of the valley floor, surrounded by transport trucks and the occasional decrepit jeep. Delgado's stronghold was still intact. She wanted to breathe a sigh of relief, but was too busy breathing period.

Josh rolled over to check behind them and swore softly. He was no tracker, but a child could have followed the trail they'd left. Suddenly, he swore again, but loudly.

"What's the matter?" She scooted closer, narrowing her eyes and peering into the far distance.

Low-hanging clouds scudded across the sunset colors of mauve and purple dipping down to meet the lacy treetops rising from the mountainous terrain. Past the forest, the savanna stretched eastward into dusk and darkness, a rippling plain of burnished grass. She scanned the view, looking for and not finding whatever had triggered his anger.

"Get down," he ordered. "Cardena got his truck going. He followed us."

Uttering a choice phrase in Spanish, Nikki flattened herself into the dirt.

He snorted in disgust. "You still swear like a drunken sailor."

She threw him an irritated glance. It was a little late for him to start policing her mouth.

"You should have outgrown that kind of language by now," he added.

Her irritation gave way to disbelief. "You haven't."

He lowered the binoculars a fraction of an inch and leveled flinty blue eyes at her. "We're not discussing me."

"Now, there's an idea," she shot back. "When did you decide to take my advice and finally learn Spanish?"

Turning away from her, he settled the binoculars back over his eyes. "A couple of years ago."

"Why?"

"I got tired of Washington."

"And you couldn't make it back here without me," she finished for him. She stated the truth bluntly, without a trace of satisfaction or the triumph she'd sworn on a long-ago night would be hers. His tense silence prompted her to continue. "I never did understand how you grew up on the Rio Grande without knowing at least conversational Spanish. What did your parents do, Josh? Keep you locked up?"

"They did what they thought was right," he said, biting off the words.

"What do you—"

"Lord, Nikki!" he interrupted, dropping the binoculars to his chest. "Didn't you ever look at me? Joshua Rios! Black hair, dark skin, and *blue* eyes?"

"Of course I've looked at you!" she blustered in self-defense. "I spent a year of my life looking at you!"

"And you still don't get it?"

"Get what?"

"Prejudice." He spat the word out, as if it left a bad taste in his mouth. "My maternal and paternal grandparents have never been in the same room together. Not for my mom and dad's wedding, not for my christening or for any of my brothers' or sisters' christenings." He put the binoculars back to his face, effectively hiding any emotion his memories might have caused.

"So you put cotton in your ears to make your mom's folks happy?" His explanation had quite a few holes in it as far as she could tell, unless his parents really had locked him up and put blinders on him.

"I didn't have to. There was enough insulating cotton in our very exclusive neighborhood and in my very exclusive private schools to keep the taint of the barrio off me. Nobody ever mistook me for a wetback . . . except once."

The edge in his voice caused her glance to go directly to the pale scar tracing his hairline. "They don't teach knife-fighting in private schools, do they?"

"No. They don't." His tone said "Let it drop," but she'd been too curious, too concerned, about that thin white line to back off when she was this close.

"Did it hurt?"

"Not at the time." He let out a labored sigh. "I was too damn scared. I thought they were going to cut my throat."

"How many were there?"

"Three. One to hold my legs, one to hold my arms, and one to slice me up. They weren't much older than I was, just a group of teenagers from the barrio with no place to go but down. They thought I was a Mexican putting on airs in my fancy clothes, hanging around with a bunch of white kids."

"I'm sorry, Josh," she whispered, wanting to reach out and touch him, to comfort the boy he no longer was.

"As I recall, you weren't there." The binoculars

came down to reveal a wry grin. "If you had been, I'm sure you wouldn't have gone running off like my prep-school buddies."

The words were no sooner out of his mouth than the truth struck him like a lightning bolt. Nikki *wouldn't* have run off and left him alone. She'd have fought them tooth and nail, verbally abused them into shame, kicked and clawed. She never would have left him alone in that alley with three boys who were bigger than both of them.

The anger he'd been nurturing with every lie she fed him slowly melted away, leaving him open to all the better memories and stronger feelings she inspired.

"You're the best friend I ever had," he admitted softly. *And the only woman I want. What am I going to do, Nikki?*

She read everything in the shadowed depths of his eyes, the honesty of what he'd said, and the pain of what he hadn't said. Sometimes it hurt to know someone so well. She tore her gaze away. She didn't know where they would go from there, except to Sulaco and betrayal.

"Is he coming this way?" She lifted her head to look in the direction of the road.

Reluctantly he followed her lead out of the dangerous emotional ground. Whatever happened between them wasn't going to happen on that rocky hilltop.

The binoculars framed the patch of road below them where her Chevy and Cardena's truck were parked. Or rather, where Cardena's truck had been parked. Josh swung the binoculars up the road and caught a dust plume arcing up behind the rapidly moving vehicle. The rancher was driving as he had earlier, like a man with someone hot on his tail.

Josh refocused on the Chevy just as a convoy of

jeeps pulled up in a cloud of flying dirt and skidding tires. The peaceful quiet of the mountain made an eerie backdrop for the commotion he witnessed. Men scrambled out of the vehicles, guns at the ready. One man directed them all with flailing arms and barked orders. Brazia.

A sick feeling worked its way up from the pit of his stomach when he saw what the men were doing to Nikki's car. "Is your insurance paid up on the Chevy?"

"Yes," she said warily.

"Well, get ready for a helluva show." He slipped the strap over his head and packed the binoculars away in his satchel.

"What do you mean?"

In answer, he nodded toward the road.

Nikki waited, her anxiety increasing with each passing minute. A tickling stream of sweat ran down the side of her face. She brushed her cheek and kept staring at the line of trees bordering the road.

"I've changed my mind about the border, Nikki. We're going to need more than a political boundary to discourage Brazia. Even the artillery in Sulaco might not be enough. The man is overly enthusiastic."

"Brazia's down there?"

"Frothing at the mouth," he added, alluding to the man's "mad dog" reputation. "Just to satisfy my curiosity"—he paused for a moment, his voice unsure—"will you tell me what you did to get so many people so damn mad at you?"

There it was, her chance to come clean, and she wasn't quite ready for it. "I don't think Cardena is mad at me," she hedged.

"Sure, Nikki. He was shooting at us because we skipped out on breakfast."

"Maybe he just wanted us to stop running."

"A couple of bullets in the back would have accomplished that real successfully," he said dryly.

"What I mean is, if he's involved with the rebels, if the phone call was to Delgado, then he might have wanted to escort us."

"That's a lot of 'ifs' and 'mights' to be hanging your life on. You won't mind if I don't buy them all, will you?"

No, she didn't mind, but she'd been doing some thinking, and—

"Carlos Delgado?" he interrupted her train of thought, his abrupt tone telling her there was more than curiosity behind the question.

"Yes. He's the one trying to unite all the different—"

"He's your boyfriend," he cut her off again, the sparks of anger returning to his eyes. "For crying out loud, Nikki, the man's old enough to be your father! Your grandfather! What in the hell is the attraction? What has he got that—" His mouth snapped shut.

"He's not my—" Her words were lost, drowned out by a massive explosion on the road. Her mouth agape, she stared in amazement at the fireball climbing into the sky. Pieces of metal and rubber floated in the air, held weightless for an instant by the force propelling them off the ground.

"The man's got a real serious streak of mayhem in him," Josh said softly, watching with equal amazement.

"He blew up my car," she gasped. "He *blew up* my car!"

"And wishes you were in it. Come on." He stood up, pulling her with him. "We've got to find a place to hide before dark."

Dazed by Brazia's single-minded viciousness, Nikki

stumbled after Josh, glancing back every now and then to watch the smoky remains of the explosion trail across the sky and become lost in the clouds. The man was insane. If he caught up with them before they reached Sulaco, he'd kill them whether they surrendered or not. The cold realization put strength into tired muscles and a tight cramp into her stomach.

Josh kept to the Sulaco side of the ridge until the increasing steepness forced them up on top. Nikki didn't question his avoidance of the forest. She didn't want to go back into the sweltering sauna of biting insects and thorny bushes either, and they were making much better time on the cliffs.

Twilight spread across the eastern sky, reaching out to meet them. The moon hung above the savanna before beginning its nightly climb over the mountains. Nikki focused all of her attention on the pale silver disk, praying she could keep going as long as Josh asked her to.

But her body reached a point of no return, and there wasn't a damn thing she could do about it.

"Josh," she hissed, doubling over, her arms wrapped around her waist.

He heard the distress in her voice and immediately came back for her. He didn't need to ask what the problem was. "We're almost to the river. Can you make it?"

"No."

He accepted the statement for what it was, her bottom line. He put his arms around her and helped her to the ground. "I'm going to find a place with better cover. Eat something while I'm gone, something besides antacid tablets."

"Sure," she groaned, pulling her legs close to her chest.

"And don't ball up." He stretched her legs out. "Breathe deep. Concentrate. Relax."

"Yes, Dr. Rios."

"And keep your wisecracks to yourself." He finished untying the sleeping bag from her duffel and stuffed it behind her back. "I won't be gone long. If you hear anybody coming, disappear." He gave her a quick, perfunctory kiss on the top of her head—which she could no sooner explain than anything else about the last twenty-four hours—and melted into the night, a shadow of dark clothes and light steps.

Nikki propped herself more securely against a boulder with the sleeping bag for a cushion. Sounds she hadn't noticed while running rose softly from the forest, wind rustling the leaves, the intermittent squawks of birds settling in, and if she cocked her head just right, the flowing rhythm of the river far below her perch.

Behind her, she heard nothing. Forcing a deep breath from her lungs, she concentrated on relaxing her body, knowing her mind was doomed to remain in a tangle of tension and readiness until . . . A mental image flickered across her mind, drawing down the corners of her mouth. Until the meeting in Sulaco, until Josh really did walk out of her life, never to reappear.

Travinas had put her in a no-win situation, but she was the one who had decided to rely on the expediency of lies. The truth wouldn't have changed anything. Brazia had been more in control of the sequence of events than either she or Josh. They'd been reacting, scrambling to stay one step ahead of him. But she knew why and Josh didn't.

She lowered her head into her hands. She should have told him. No, she reconsidered immediately.

There was no telling what direction he would have taken off in if he'd known Brazia was searching for him. He certainly wouldn't have chosen to go to Sulaco, where *she* needed him to be.

Lost in her own guilty thoughts, she didn't hear the stealthy footsteps creeping up behind her. And by the time she saw the Kalashnikov leveled at her face, it was far too late.

# *Eleven*

*Overkill,* Nikki thought, working up her anger to hold back the fear pushing at her from every corner of her mind. Her captors had bound, gagged, and blindfolded her before dragging her off the mountain and throwing her in the back of a jeep. She strained against the cords tying her wrists and tried not to imagine what it was she tasted on the rag crammed into her mouth. Oil or axle grease, maybe. Unsanitary, definitely.

The careening vehicle swayed into a turn, and she braced her feet to hold herself upright on the backseat. Pinpricks of dust and fine gravel stung her face and arms. The curses she couldn't speak caught in her throat.

They wouldn't kill her, she kept telling herself. Travinas wanted Joshua Rios, not Nikki Kydd, and Josh was long gone, probably halfway to Sulaco by now. He was probably worried sick, or thanking his lucky stars he'd gotten rid of her. She should have told him; she should have told him everything. She bit down on the rag and strained again, rubbing her wrists up and down. If Brazia caught up with him, Josh wouldn't have a chance. *Damn those ropes!* She grunted, giving it everything she had, then slumped back into the seat, the ropes still securely tied.

They might try using her for bait, to draw Josh out. What an ironic twist that would be. She'd baited her trap with him but ended up catching herself a whole bunch of trouble. Suddenly the cord slipped a little lower on her wrists, giving her hope and fear at the same time. Even if she worked herself free, she'd be helpless against so many.

*They might kill me.*

The thought she'd been fighting crept in softly ahead of her anger, chilling her despite the sultriness of the night. They'd caught her within shouting distance of Sulaco. Travinas wasn't stupid. He'd probably already put the pieces together: Delgado slipping through his fingers in the nick of time, Josh showing up at her apartment, the two of them heading north. Sweat broke out on her upper lip, and she tried to wipe it off with her shoulder. How long had they been driving? Half an hour? Longer?

She wished they hadn't blindfolded her. It was too dramatic, too scary, too reminiscent of firing squads and last requests.

The jeep took another turn and slowed down. Nikki's heart started pounding faster. Reckoning time.

When they stopped, someone hauled her out of the jeep, using the nape of her neck and the waistband of her pants for handholds. She landed on her knees, and the same someone immediately picked her up again, half dragging, half carrying her forward.

She stumbled along until he jerked her to a stop and pulled the blindfold down around her neck. The first thing she saw, the only thing she saw, was Brazia, standing in the glare of the headlights, his black gaze raking her with satisfied contempt.

"Journalists are such fools. And you, Nikki Kydd, are the biggest fool of all." His lips curled around the words. A riding crop twitched in his hand. "I told Travinas to get rid of you a long time ago. Now I'll get rid of you myself. He can thank me later. Lock her up." He dismissed the soldier by cracking the tiny whip against his thigh.

Her protests died in the greasy rag over her mouth. She gave in to panic and struggled against the hands gripping her arms, propelling her toward a shack at the edge of the forest. She kicked the soldier in the shin, and he twisted her arms up between her shoulderblades. She groaned at the pain. Then she was on her face in the dirt inside the shack. The door slammed shut behind her. A bolt slid into place.

Her breath came hard between sobs of agony and fear. Using her shoulder for leverage, she inched her knees under her. She had to get out of there, before Brazia—

A scuffling sound from the other side of the shack froze her in a crouch. "Nikki?"

*Josh!*

He came out of the corner, a looming shadow against the barred window. "Dammit! Just a second." He twisted his shoulders, muscles straining against his bonds. With a grunt he broke free, shaking the rope from his hands. He dropped to his knees and untied the gag from her mouth.

"How did you do that?" she asked, working the kinks out of her jaw, relief flooding her veins. Josh was there. They'd think of something. They had to or they'd both be dead.

"I didn't give the guy who tied me up a chance to

do it right," he muttered, scooting behind her and unraveling the knot at her wrists.

In a minute she was free. She threw her arms around him and held on for dear life, burying her head in the crook of his neck. "Oh, Josh . . . Josh." All of her love came out in the breathless whisper of his name.

"Nikki, Nikki," he parodied, roughly pulling her arms away and setting her back on her heels. "I'll be damned if I let you get around me again, so save the theatrics."

"Wh-what?"

"Not quite," he growled. "Try 'why.' As in why do you want me dead? Three years is a helluva long time to carry a grudge."

"What are you talking about?"

"Brazia. He congratulated me on having stayed a step ahead of him since Colombia. He told me about your deal with Travinas, and he promised me neither of us would see the light of day. Interesting story, except the ending needs a little work." He finished with a disgusted sound and pushed himself up, slapping the dust off his pants. He walked as far away from her as the small building allowed. "So what do you think, Nikki? Will your boyfriend come to the rescue? Or have you lied and cheated your way out of his affections, too?"

Stunned, Nikki sat in the dirt, her mind a complete blank.

"Is that a yes?" He half turned and looked at her over his shoulder, one eyebrow lifted in a sardonic curve. "You should have been smarter, Nikki. Old men are a lot harder to fool than young men. They like their little girls all sweet and compliant." He laughed softly and shook his head, his gaze raking her body before he met her eyes with a bitter look.

"Ah, you're sweet, Nikki. Plenty sweet. But compliance has never been your strong point. . . . *Damn you.*" The last disappeared in a harsh whisper as he turned back to the window. He grabbed the iron bars and gave them a mighty shake.

Nikki watched his fruitless efforts, and without wanting to, she imagined those big hands around her neck, throttling her.

"You're wrong," she said, using all of her courage to speak.

"Save it for Delgado." He whirled away from the window, his gaze searching the shack.

"He's not interested in my opinions."

"No." He laughed again, a dry, mirthless sound. "I don't suppose he is."

Her face burned at the crude twist he'd put on her words. She'd had enough. She pushed herself to her feet, sick and tired of being in the dirt, of being called a liar, and of taking the blame for every damn thing that had gone wrong.

"No, he's not!" she sputtered, taking a step forward. "The only thing I've got that anybody in this whole damn country wants is you! You and whatever it is you've got stored up in that thick skull of yours! What in the hell did *I* do?" Her voice rose along with her eyebrows. "The question is what in the hell did *you* do? Brazia wants you dead. Travinas wants you any way he can get you, and the only way I could get Delgado to even *talk* to me was to promise I'd bring you to him!"

"Stop shouting," he said, moving toward her.

"I'll shout if I want—"

He clapped a hand over her mouth. "No, you won't. Now listen to me, Nikki, and listen good." She pushed at his hand, and he swung her back against his chest. His other arm snaked around her waist, holding her in a relentless grip. He lowered his mouth to her ear and whispered, "There are fifteen soldiers and one crazed colonel out there. The only chance we've got is to keep whatever information we have to ourselves. Brazia doesn't know about your personal involvement with Delgado, and that's our ace in the hole." He paused for the space of several heartbeats, his breath rasping against her cheek, the tension and strength in his body overwhelming her feeble attempts at escape. When he spoke again, his voice was rough and low. "God knows if you were mine, I wouldn't let that butcher have you."

Nikki's hands tightened on his arm, but to hold him there, not to push him away. Her eyes drifted closed on a shuddered sigh. She wanted to turn around and fold herself into his arms and tell him she was his, that she had always and only been his.

But he wouldn't believe her, not now. He'd think she was trying to cover herself one more time.

Her head dropped in weariness. She pushed his hands away and walked over to the window. She'd brought them to this, and he had to know the truth. "There won't be any rescue, Josh. Delgado won't come. Not for me."

"Why not? What did you do to him?" Josh frowned. If she'd pushed Delgado even half as hard as she'd been pushing him, he wouldn't blame the guy for giving up on her. But to abandon her to Brazia? No man would do that.

"It's more like what I didn't do." Her voice drifted back into the room. "I never slept with him, not that he asked. Our relationship is strictly business, and our bargain is simple: I bring you in and he keeps you in one piece."

A long silence greeted her confession, and Nikki could almost hear him adding up the damning facts one by one and coming up with betrayal. A knot of pain began curling and cramping in her stomach. She'd never had a chance. Travinas had outmaneuvered her at every turn.

"How many people did you sell me out to?" The edge in his voice cut through the tension like a razor.

Nikki gave a slight shake of her head, more a denial of his hate than of his words. By lying to him she had sold him out, but what did it matter anymore? Brazia had them now.

"Do you know why they want me?" he asked.

"The story you have on Travinas."

"And you're working all the sides toward the middle." He muttered something obscene, something she wished she hadn't heard, and something, oh, so true. "What do you get out of all of this, besides the front-page spread Travinas gave you?"

"My mother."

"What?"

"My mother," she said louder, forcing herself to face him. "The woman you wanted me to leave three years ago. She's dying, Josh, and I want her out of prison before that happens."

He stared at her, what was left of his emotions icing over into glacial status. He didn't believe her, didn't dare or want to believe her. But the summery green eyes meeting his weren't lying now. A hurtful breath caught in his throat. She'd made her choice. A muscle twitched in his cheek at his effort to keep the pain off his face.

"One life for another, Nikki?" He finally found the awful words. "Pretty nasty business, isn't it?"

She lifted her hands in a helpless, pleading gesture, knowing there was no way to make the truth less mercenary. "Brazia was going to kill you, whether you surrendered or not. I thought if I got to you before he did, I could keep you alive."

"By hand-delivering me?" He'd meant to make the words sound scornful, but a measure of his pain got through, making him even madder. When she tried to speak, he cut her off. "Shut up!" He needed to think. He needed to get out of there. But the confusion and hurt filling his mind made it impossible to think. She'd suckered him royally! He paced the shack, working himself into a frenzy, his body shaking. When he couldn't take it anymore, he turned on her.

"God, Nikki! When did you become such a heartless bitch! After you left me? Or was the whole year a lie?"

His words hurt her more than a physical blow. She felt them slice through her body.

Her hand slipped around one of the window bars, and she held on tight. "I'll get you out of here, Josh," she said, her knees weak, her voice wavering. "I promise."

"How?" he yelled, forgetting the need to be quiet. "From what I've heard, Brazia doesn't like girls!"

She flinched, but let the slur slide. She didn't rate too high on her own list, either. "I'll give him Delgado. I know the rebels' strength and enough of Delgado's plans to buy your freedom."

*And my mother's.* Politics didn't have a place in her heart anymore. She didn't care who ran San Simeon as long as she got what she wanted. She'd use them all, play them all against one another, the whole power-crazed lot of them. She just wanted Josh and her mother out of it.

"No, Nikki." He shook his head, his expression reflecting the cold fury in his eyes.

"I'll make Brazia give you a jeep." She talked over

his dissent. "Head for the border. Don't go to Sulaco. If he acts on my information—"

"You always did think too fast for your own good."

"—there won't be anything left of the place by tomorrow afternoon."

"So quit thinking and give me a chance to figure out what we're going to do!" Lord, what a fool he was, he thought. What did she have to do? Actually put the knife in his back before he could walk away from her?

Maybe, he admitted, knowing it didn't matter one way or the other. He wasn't going anywhere without her, not tonight. He'd either get her out or make sure they both got shot trying. He hadn't used the term "butcher" lightly, and Brazia *didn't* like women. He'd seen the mad dog's handiwork once out on the savanna. He wouldn't let Brazia do that to Nikki.

"Okay," he said, "here's the plan. When they come to get us, I'll distract the guards and you make a run for it."

"That's crazy. I'm talking to Brazia."

"Do you *really* think he's just going to let me drive out of here?"

"He might! Which is more of a chance than you've got of overpowering fifteen soldiers with guns!"

"No!" Brazia would love having her grovel at his feet, and her subservience would only make him crueler. Damn her. She couldn't even betray him without screwing it up. If she'd been sleeping with Delgado, he would have come to save her. Any man she gave her love to would risk his life for her. He didn't have to look any further than himself to know the truth. Fool! Delgado had been their last hope.

Nikki opened her mouth, then snapped it shut. There was no reasoning with him.

They glared at each other across the shack, the

full moon lighting their standoff with its pale silvery glow. Nikki gave in first, her gaze dropping to the dirt floor and the striped shadows cast by the iron bars over the window. Her eyes flicked back up to his.

"I tried it," he said. "Remember? Those bars are sunk into cement."

She glanced around the four bare walls of the shack. There was nothing, absolutely nothing inside except two people desperate to get out.

"The door?" she asked.

"Kicking it out, even supposing I could, would be an invitation to get our heads blown off. They're camped right out front, probably digging our graves."

He didn't want to push the minute of dying any closer than it already was, but she deserved to know how bad things really were. Yet she didn't deserve to know how much worse they could be. Not for him; Brazia would shoot him without a second glance. Nikki was the one who would suffer.

And maybe, just maybe, he'd get lucky. One small miracle lasting a few seconds might mean the difference between life and death.

"Graves?" Nikki repeated weakly, the full impact of their situation hitting home with that one word.

"Brazia's standard operating procedure. San Simeon is one big shallow grave from the mountains to Costa Rica. Mostly penny-ante drug dealers trying to take a cut out of Travinas's lifeline. He's never allowed Brazia to execute foreigners before, especially reporters, but you and I don't fall into that category anymore."

"Wh-what category are we in?" They both still worked for internationally renowned newspapers. They both still carried press identification.

"Sorry, Nikki," he said, watching her scramble the

facts around, trying to come up with an answer. "I gave up my immunity the first time I stepped into the middle of Travinas's cocaine ring, and you gave up yours when you decided to play his game by his rules."

Frightened eyes locked onto his. "There has to be some way out, Josh! We can't just stand here waiting! We have to . . . to . . ." She wrapped her arms around her waist, tighter and tighter, trying to still the panicked beating of her pulse. *Graves.* She squeezed her eyes shut to block the image, but blackness only made it clearer—a dark hole in the ground, filled by their cold, crumpled bodies. Then his arms were around her, and he was warm and strong, with life flowing through him. "Josh, I have to talk to him. I have to try."

Remorse and self-loathing flooded him as he held her, feeling her fear, the trembling of her body. His chest swelled with a deep breath, and he measured his words carefully. "Nikki? Brazia doesn't want Delgado, even if you could deliver him on a silver platter. Delgado doesn't matter. This isn't about politics. It's about power and money and hurting people. I'm—I'm sorry you got involved. I should have realized it all came down to me and not you."

And he should have. Days ago in Panama, he should have read further between the lines and not have let his memories and his love get in the way. Brazia might have cut him down with a bullet in the back, but Nikki would have been out of it, a useless pawn. Her mother would have died, but her mother was going to die anyway. "God, Nikki, I'm sorry." His voice broke with all the pain he felt for her, for all the battles she'd fought and lost, for the young life she might lose that night.

Her arms went around his waist, and he felt her

tears soak through his shirt and brand his chest. The slender body in his arms shook with silent sobs.

He looked down at the tangled mass of her hair, at the dirt streaking her cheeks, and his heart broke with wanting her, with wanting to erase the bleakness from her life. "I should never have let you get away from me."

Filled with sadness and acceptance, she lifted her eyes to meet his. "It's too late for regrets, Josh."

"It's never too late for regrets, or mine would have gone away a long time ago. But they didn't go away, Nikki, and I came back to find out why."

"And that's the biggest regret of all."

"No, *querida*," he said, his voice hoarse. "This is the biggest regret."

With one fluid movement, he tilted her head back and sealed his mouth over hers. The muscles in his arms bunched and flexed to hold her closer, and closer still, until her soft curves were laminated against his body from chest to thigh. Her lips parted, granting him the entry he sought with the teasing track of his tongue.

The heat he found in her kiss put the night to shame. She clung to him, pushing him quickly to the edge of reason. An inexorable tightening wound its way through his body, urged on by her soft whimpers and the desperate grasp of her hands on his shoulders.

"I love you, Nikki," he murmured, holding her tighter. When she lifted her face, he sealed his vow with another kiss, a kiss of sweetness, longing, and more regret than he thought he could bear.

Then their time together was over. The door swung open with a bang, revealing four soldiers with four guns, all of them pointed at Nikki's back.

Josh wanted to shout and throw himself against

the guards. He wanted to create the melee he'd promised, to instigate a shooting spree. But his instinct to protect her was too strong to be overridden by his horrifyingly logical plan. He stepped in front of her, and the soldiers moved inside, surrounding them. One of the men reached for Nikki, but before he could touch her, Josh lashed out with his fist. He connected once, then doubled over with a groan, clutching his stomach where a soldier had buried the butt end of his machine gun. Another blow cracked against the back of his neck and dropped him to his knees.

Pain exploded in his head, fire bursts of light and wells of darkness pleading with him to black out, to slip into the peace of oblivion. He fought the temptation with every ounce of strength he had, forcing his eyes to open and his breath to keep coming.

"Josh!" Her voice came from a great distance, adding her strength to his. With a groan, he struggled to his feet.

In two languages and in a hundred different ways, Nikki told the soldiers what she thought of their combined manhood, rattling off a stream of invective guaranteed to scorch their ears. She whirled on each of them in turn, personally including them in her verbal rampage.

The youngest soldier giggled nervously, and Nikki knew he'd never heard such language come out of a woman's mouth. But the novelty was short-lived.

"*Cállate! Basta, ya!*" One of the others shouted her into silence.

Pushing and shoving with their guns, the soldiers prodded them outside into the night. One of the men stooped down and picked up the blindfold and gag Josh had taken off her. Nikki caught the quick action out of the corner of her eye, and her fury skittered into a wall of dread. They were going to die in darkness.

Her mouth went dry. Her life tried to pass before her eyes, but it was too soon. There was too much fear and not enough acceptance of the inevitable. She turned to Josh, her mind groping for answers she'd never find. The guards had already wrapped the blindfold over his eyes and were tying his hands behind him. The light offered by the cooking fire showed a sticky mass of blood and hair at the nape of his neck—the last thing she saw.

The blindfold came around her face, tied and tightened by hands that didn't care. Someone else jerked her arms behind her back and knotted a rope around her wrists. The guards pushed her forward and down onto her knees.

"Hurry, hurry . . . No! I'll kill them myself!"

*Brazia.* Nikki recognized his voice, then immediately tried to shake his image from her mind. She didn't want her last thought to be of the mad dog.

*Last thought!* Where was Josh? A groan and the force of someone hitting the ground close to her telegraphed his presence.

"Start my jeep!" Brazia shouted.

Nikki heard a clip snap into a gun. The night was moving too fast. *Hurry, hurry.* Brazia's voice echoed in her ears. A trembling from deep inside shook her body. She tried to speak Josh's name, but she couldn't form the word and hyperventilate at the same time, and hyperventilation was winning hands down. Her whirling thoughts careened out of control. She was going to die scared senseless. Not even the pressure of the gun at the base of her skull brought her down to earth.

"Josh . . . Josh . . ."

Her desperate gasp tore through the air—then the shot.

Josh heard the panic in her voice, he felt and heard the explosion, the fall, and he knew the best of his life had ended.

# Twelve

Dust turned to mud in her mouth. She spat out the dirty taste and wondered why getting shot didn't hurt more where the bullet had gone in, and why she still hurt in other places like her arms and stomach. Something was wrong. Had Brazia missed? Impossible. He'd had the gun to her head.

She did a quick check of her senses and came to an undeniable conclusion: she was alive. Then why couldn't she move? The weight crushing her into the earth shifted and pushed against her, and she pushed back. The weight slid off her with a groan and a thud.

"Josh?" Her voice trembled with a terrible premonition.

"Nikki?"

She jerked her head around toward his voice. If he wasn't on top of her, who—Brazia! Someone had shot Brazia, but he wasn't dead either. She scrambled to her feet to get away from him, then immediately dropped back to the ground, suddenly aware of the chaos all around her. Shots were coming from everywhere, with her, Josh, and Brazia in the middle.

"Stay down! Stay put!" Josh yelled.

Lord, she wished she could see.

"Say something, Nikki! I can't find you!" Seconds after she fell, Josh realized help had come. One of the soldiers had literally run over him trying to escape, knocking him down and turning him around.

"Here. I'm over here." Her voice came from behind him.

Help had come in time. Nikki was alive. He prayed he could keep her that way.

Shuffling on his knees, he scooted closer to her. "Are you hurt?"

"No. Brazia's here. He's alive, but I think he's been shot."

"Good," he said, his breath coming hard from fear, the shock of thinking she'd been shot, and the sheer relief of knowing she was alive. "Lie down and roll close to my back." He nudged her shoulder and felt her drop to the ground. Bullets whizzed by them, pinging off the vehicles parked haphazardly around the compound. Someone screamed.

Nikki shivered at the sound of terror cutting across the compound. A minute ago it could have been her death cry, or Josh's. It might still be.

"Can you reach my hands?" he asked urgently.

"Yes." She understood what he wanted, and she worked frantically at the ropes tying his hands, her movements hindered by her own bound wrists.

When he was free, he rolled over, ripping off his blindfold and hers. He reached for her hands. "We'll try for the forest, see who comes out on top in this thing. Come on."

The rope fell away. Cradling her arms, she got to her knees. A fresh round of gunfire put her right back flat on the ground. She pulled herself closer to Josh, until their shoulders touched. Feathers of dust skittered across the compound on all sides of them.

"We're pinned," she gasped, her fingers digging into the dirt, her heart racing.

"Yeah." Josh lifted his head a fraction of an inch and glanced around. He couldn't tell the bad guys from the good guys, or if there were any good guys.

A fireball streaked out of the night on his left, sucking up the oxygen with a whoosh and blinding him with a red-orange burst of light. No explosion rocked the air, just a sudden intense heat coming out of nowhere and destroying the shack. Fire crawled down the building and into the forest.

He wiped the sweat out of his eyes and watched their escape route go up in flames. Damn, he wished they were anywhere else in the world. He jerked his head around, looking for an alternative. "Try for Brazia's jeep. Belly-crawl." That was the best he could come up with.

Pushing with her elbows and knees, Nikki wriggled forward. The jeep was ahead of her, the four tires marking a safety zone of shadow in the torched battlefield. Yellow and red firelight ringed the north border of the camp. Whoever had come after Brazia was using the mad dog's own tricks against him— saturation violence and mayhem. They were going to crush him, and maybe crush her and Josh in the bargain.

She slid the last foot under the jeep, pushed by Josh's hand on her bottom. Then, as suddenly as it had started, the battle was over. The *pop-pop* of the final rifle shots faded into the crashing sounds of the tumbling, flaming shack. Voices came out of the darkness, shouted orders and cheers of victory. From their hiding place beneath the jeep, Nikki saw a man push Brazia's body with his booted foot. Brazia cringed.

"He's alive," the man announced to his troops. "Take him to Sulaco, *inmediatamente!*"

Two soldiers hurried forward to haul the colonel away. The man turned, and the lights of the fire lit his face with a flickering crimson glow.

"Cardena," she whispered, glancing at Josh. "He came back for us."

"Yeah, but why?" Josh had been used, abused, and double-crossed too many times in the last thirty-six hours to accept anything or anybody at face value. Not Luis Cardena . . . and not Nikki Kydd, not any longer.

"To take us to Delgado?" she offered, her voice catching on every other breath, like his own.

He squeezed his eyes shut. Some things would never change, he thought, and Nikki drawing trouble like a magnet was the worst of those things. Yes, he loved her. Yes, he accepted the responsibility for being the partial cause of her involvement. But there was something about Nikki, and Nikki alone, that lit fuses and created sparks wherever she went. The woman should be under lock and key. She was dangerous, and he'd had his fill of danger. She'd used him in the worst possible way, and although he understood her reasons, he hoped that somewhere deep down inside himself there was a self-defense mechanism to protect him from being hurt further by her. If he sat tight and waited, maybe it would kick in and he'd be able to think straight.

With the unsettling facts firmly planted in his mind, he opened his eyes and stared for a long moment at his hands. Nothing happened. He'd run out of time, and they'd run out of choices.

"Okay, Nikki. The only way we're going to find out is to ask and hope we like the answer, because we sure as hell aren't going to get out of here without him noticing." Pushing himself out from under the jeep, he deliberately refrained from looking at her, at the most appealing face he'd ever seen. Even when it was smudged with dirt and framed by sweaty, stringy hair, he was a fool for that face.

Nikki followed, unsure of what emotion she'd seen in his eyes. Resignation, definitely. But sadness too? By her reckoning the worst was over. She was still shaking, inside and out, but they were both in one piece, Brazia had been neutralized, and Travinas had to deal with her now. She held the winning hand again, if she had the strength to keep her players in line, to keep Josh by her side—the strength and the sheer audacity after that terrible confession he'd wrung out of her in the shack.

Cardena's men surrounded them in a rush, grabbing them and hustling them to the middle of the compound. Neither she nor Josh put up any resistance.

"Señorita Kydd, Señor Rios," Cardena said, dropping the pretense of their lie. "You are both lucky to be alive, especially you, señorita. Another second, or a less steady hand"—he raised his rifle and leveled her with a dark-eyed glare—"and you would be meeting your Maker."

Nikki nodded her thanks and slanted a quick glance up at Josh.

"Damn good shot," Josh said, ignoring the pull of her eyes. "You missed on purpose this morning."

"It is the only way I ever miss, señor. Had you not been so eager to run, I could have saved you much unpleasantness. As it is, I will be content with saving your lives."

Josh took the wound to his pride like a man. He kept his face blank and his hands loose at his sides. He was in no mood to dish out the gratitude Cardena wanted and deserved, at least not for the night's fiasco. But Cardena had just done him another favor, one Josh would have thanked him for if the situation had allowed. He'd made Josh angry; he'd triggered the self-defense mechanism.

"I'm sure you had your reasons, or your orders," he drawled, meeting Cardena's black gaze with a challenge of his own.

"Both," Cardena slowly admitted, the barest hint of a smile touching the corner of his mouth. "It seems, Señor Rios, that you are a person of much value. Carlos Delgado is convinced you have something he needs."

"But does he have anything I need?"

Cardena's gaze flicked over Nikki before coming back to Josh. "That depends on how you value the lady and her happiness."

Slowly but surely Nikki felt herself being cut out of the deal. All she'd ever had was Josh to bargain with. She was only the liaison between him and Travinas, between him and Delgado. He didn't need her. She needed him. Everybody needed him.

"Josh?" She touched his arm, gazing up at him. She knew it would be so easy for him to walk away, for she certainly hadn't given him any reason not to. Quite the contrary, she'd given him every reason to leave and never look back. No, never look back—the way he thought she'd left him.

Josh stared down at her, at her pale face and the look of desperate uncertainty in her eyes. Three years of loneliness had brought him to this moment, three years of missing her with an ache he hadn't been able to assuage. Two days of pure hell hadn't changed the emotional reality of his love, his loneliness, or the ache. If anything, he missed her more now, for the young girl he'd loved so completely was truly lost to him. A week ago, the woman waiting for his answer had made her decision. One life for another. He wouldn't deny her.

"Take me to Delgado," he said to Cardena. "For the price of Helen Cavazos's freedom, I'll tell him what he needs to know to bring Travinas down."

He felt Nikki's fingers tighten on his arm. "Thank you." Her voice was soft, almost too soft to hear.

He ignored her and continued speaking directly to Cardena. If he stopped now, he might not have the courage to say what he still had to say. "There is one other condition. Nicolita Kydd. I won't tell Delgado anything until she's out of the country."

"Señor?" Cardena's glance traveled between the two of them.

"You heard me. I want her gone, and I want you to take her. Whatever arrangements have to be made for Helen's release can be done without Nikki. That's the deal."

That was the deal, and that was the end of it, he thought, strangely relieved by the simplicity of the plan. He wasn't up to complications of any sort, physical, mental, or emotional. His body was bruised, his mind even more so by Brazia's revelations and Nikki's confession, by the horror he'd felt when he thought she'd died. He never wanted to feel that kind of pain again. It was unbearable. No, he shouldn't have let her get away from him, but neither should she have asked him to come back.

"I don't have the authority to—"

"Take it," Josh interrupted, calling Cardena's bluff. The man had needed plenty of authority to pull off the raid. "Take her. Or Delgado can wait until I get back from taking her myself."

"Where?"

"The States."

"No. No, Rios." Cardena shook his head, becoming agitated. "We—the revolution, Delgado—none of us can wait that long. The schedule has been set.

The country will be freed in two—soon, very soon,"
he corrected himself. "Delgado wants to give your
information to the people immediately after he gains
control."

"Then take her," Josh demanded.

"Maybe one of my men—"

"You, Cardena. Only you. You're the one who saved
her life. You're the one I want to take her out of
here, tonight." He didn't want time for anything else
to go wrong, for Travinas to marshal his forces, for
Delgado to change his mind. He didn't want time to
think about her leaving. He wanted time to heal,
alone, knowing she was safe.

Nikki heard the conversation through a haze of
shock, her initial relief dying like the flames coming
up against the damp forest floor. Josh was sending
her away, and Cardena was going to let him. She
saw the indecision on the older man's face, but she
also saw the inevitability of his answer.

"No," she said quickly, trying to sway the odds in
her favor. She didn't want to leave him like this,
with so many things left unsaid, with their love and
friendship tainted by the ruin of her deception.

"Don't undercut yourself, Nikki." Josh looked down
at her. "For your mother's sake, you should be begging him to take you out of here. Nothing's going to
happen until you're gone."

"I'll leave. I promise. But not like this. Not tonight.
I can help you."

"I've had all the help from you I can take. No
offense"—he raised his hand to stop her protest—
"just the plain honest-to-goodness truth. You're hell
on a man, Nikki, real hell."

One look at him proved his point. Dirt and mud
covered every square inch of him. His clothes were
torn. Blood stained the collar of his shirt. And none
of it compared to the weariness in his eyes.

"I can change, Josh," she said softly, pleading with him to believe what even she doubted. She needed to change, wanted to change, but she'd been running so hard for so long, subordinating everything to one ultimate goal—her mother's freedom.

"Prove it. Leave with Cardena. When your mother is released I'll bring her to you." He turned to Cardena, not giving her a chance to say anything more. "What's your decision?"

"You've given me no choice," Cardena said. "I will take Nikki home."

"How long will it take?"

"I have connections. We can be in Miami by tomorrow afternoon."

"Miami?" Josh asked in a wary tone.

"Don't worry, Señor Rios. Not everyone in Miami deals in contraband. My connections are old and trusted family friends. She will come to no harm under my care."

"If I didn't believe you, you'd be showing up in Sulaco empty-handed instead of taking off for Florida." He dismissed Cardena and turned to Nikki. He thought about kissing her good-bye, then decided against anything as dangerous as a kiss. He thought about touching her face, her hair, then thought he'd better not. So he stood there, looking down at her, struggling with the words that wouldn't come. "Are you going to your aunt's in Colorado?" he finally asked.

"I think she's the only one in the family who'll have me." Nikki attempted a smile.

"You're a celebrity. You'll have them all eating out of your hand," he assured her with a weak smile of his own.

"I don't know, Josh. I left a long time ago. I was only fifteen the last time I saw my aunt." Her glance strayed to the toes of her tennis shoes. She hated saying good-bye, hated leaving him. "Maybe I'll go to Washington. David can put me up until I get reassigned. That is, if he doesn't fire me. I promised him I'd stay out of trouble . . . and now I'm going to miss out on the biggest story in San Simeon." Her gaze slowly rose to his, and she swore softly. "Dammit, Josh. This is practically blackmail, making me leave now."

"Priorities, Nikki, not blackmail."

"You're going to get a week's worth of front-page exclusives out of this."

"And you're going to get your mother."

"David will kill me."

"Only if Travinas doesn't get to you first."

The sobering fact hit home with the force of truth. She'd rattled the mad dog's chain, and the master wouldn't be too far behind. He'd used her, never intending to fulfill his end of their bargain. The only chance her mother had was in Delgado's victory, and Delgado needed Josh.

"I believe these belong to you." Cardena returned to them, carrying her duffel and Josh's satchel. She hadn't realized he'd left. "My men are ready. You will go with Miguel, Señor Rios. He'll take you to Delgado. And you, señorita, you will come with me back to the ranch. We'll take my plane into Costa Rica. From there I'll arrange our entry into the United States." He looked at Josh. "I'll contact you from Costa Rica, if my plans meet with your approval."

"Bring her passport back with you from Miami."

"Josh!" she gasped. He was clipping her wings but good.

"Sorry, Nikki." He lifted the satchel strap over his head and angled it across his chest. His hand automatically slipped inside the front pocket for a cheroot.

"We must go, señorita." Cardena gestured toward the jeep pulling to a stop in the middle of the compound. "*Adiós,* señor."

"*Adiós.*" Josh jammed the cheroot in his mouth and struck a match off his pants.

Cardena touched her arm, silently telling her it was time to go. She shook him off, keeping her gaze fixed on Josh. "Promise me . . . promise me you'll bring my mother to Colorado. Boulder, Colorado."

"I remember." He inhaled deeply, drawing the smoke into his mouth.

"Promise me, Josh," she insisted.

He dropped the match and removed the cheroot from between his teeth. Troubled blue eyes met hers through a cloud of slowly exhaled smoke. She read many things in his shadowed gaze, none of which she wanted to believe. The sadness she'd only guessed at before was undeniable now, the weariness even more evident.

"Promise me you'll come." This wasn't going to be their last good-bye. She wouldn't allow it.

"I'll come." He sucked again on the cheroot and blew another cloud into the air. "I promise."

# *Thirteen*

He'd lied.

Nikki tipped her sunglasses down on her nose and checked the hand-drawn street map provided to her, under duress, by a reporter at the *Times*. He'd sworn her to secrecy on his Pulitzer, promising to disavow ever having seen her should she confess where she'd gotten the map to Josh's Texas hideaway. The fishing was too good, he'd said, to risk not getting invited back.

Fishing. Nikki couldn't believe it. She'd been worrying herself sick over him for the past month, and he'd been off fishing the coastal waters of the Gulf of Mexico.

And this neighborhood. She didn't believe it either. Stately oaks, old clapboard houses set back from the street, wide lawns, flowering bushes lining the gravel driveways. The place had an aura of genteel but homey shabbiness. She'd expected something else, something more along the lines of where her aunt lived in Boulder, a modern neighborhood of glassy houses and artful landscapes, not this last bastion of middle America, not for Joshua Rios.

As if on cue, a young woman rounded the corner of one of the houses, garden basket and clippers in hand, a wide-brimmed hat shielding her face from the sun, and a toddler in tow. Nikki checked the house numbers. Josh's next-door neighbors.

Taking her foot off the brake, she eased her car down the street and pulled into his driveway. Blue hydrangeas followed the dirt and gravel lane around to the back of the white house. A garage with wide barn doors stood on the edge of the lot. The driveway continued to a gate leading to the alley. Nikki stopped the car next to the screened back porch and wished she'd called first. He'd obviously come to this backwater town to disappear for a while. Company, especially hers, might be the last thing he wanted showing up on his doorstep.

But she'd given him a month. A month she'd spent nursing and nurturing her mother back to health. He'd fulfilled that end of the bargain. He'd gotten her mother out of San Simeon. He'd helped Delgado destroy Travinas. He'd gotten his week of front-page exclusives for the *Times.*

David still wasn't speaking to her, although he had taken time to dictate her "resignation" letter. She'd signed without a fight. She was tired of fighting.

She got out of the car and shook out her calf-length white cotton skirt. Then she reached back into the car for her matching twenty-nine-cent flip-flops. After a moment's consideration, she left her duffel bag in the front seat, to save time and embarrassment if he immediately kicked her out.

She'd come this far, she told herself, eyeing the

screen door. With a steadying breath to bolster her courage, she mounted the steps and knocked on the door. When no one answered, she ventured onto the porch and tried the kitchen door. It creaked open, compliments of a faulty latch and no lock.

"Josh?" She peeked inside and called his name again. Still no answer.

She looked back out onto the porch, her gaze drifting over the hammock hanging in the corner and the Formica dinette table strewn with large fishing lures. A couple of orange life vests hung from hooks in the kitchen wall. A wilting philodendron was pushed into a corner, its vines trailing up a length of fishing line tied to the porch screen. There was nothing there to remind her of the Josh she knew, unless she counted the dusty stack of newspapers and magazines next to the dying plant. It made her wonder just how well she did know him. It made her wonder what she was doing there.

Sighing, she turned around, her flip-flops squeaking on the floorboards. Their time together had always been so intense, so fraught with tight deadlines, fast-breaking stories, and then the final disastrous two days. She still woke up in the middle of the night sometimes, covered with sweat, her breath caught in her throat, still feeling the remembered pressure of a gun at the base of her skull.

Cardena had made a worse deal than he'd thought when he'd agreed to take her home. Halfway over the Caribbean, she'd come out of shock, surprising both of them with a near-hysterical collapse. The man was a saint. He'd talked with her, reassured her, listened to her babbling and crying, and in the end, he'd traveled with her all the way to Boulder, personally taking her to her aunt's house. Saying good-bye to him had been almost as hard as leaving Josh.

Almost, but not quite, which was why she found herself standing on this old back porch near the Texas-Louisiana state line. She lifted the hair off the back of her neck and looked around again. As long as he wasn't there, he couldn't kick her out. She might as well get comfortable.

The moon sat cool and serene in the darkening rainbow of the sky, adding its clear light to the warm, humid night. Josh stopped his car halfway up the driveway and walked around the front of the house to get the mail. He picked the evening paper up off the front porch and scanned the headlines while letting himself in the door.

Once inside, he tossed the paper on the couch and started stripping his shirt off over his head. That was when he noticed the kitchen light. More curious than wary, and realizing it should have been the other way around, he went to investigate.

He could have left the beer bottle on the table, he admitted, and the back door did have a tendency to swing open in the slightest breeze unless it was hooked from the inside, but the sunglasses on the counter definitely didn't belong to him. They were big and pink, and they were nested around a half-eaten roll of antacid tablets. A thrill of excitement he couldn't control curled around the pit of his stomach. *She's here.*

He crossed the room, instinctively heading for the coolest spot in the house. Shaded from the moon and the sunset by large overhanging trees, the porch was dark except for the narrow beam of light coming from the kitchen. The yellow band streamed across the floor, split by his shadow as he opened the door wider.

He stood there for a long time, leaning against the jamb and resting his head on his arm, watching her sleep in the hammock. A feeling of deep, unexplainable peace washed over him. He seemed to have spent so much of his life thinking about her. In the last month he'd come close to convincing himself she was nothing more than a strange infatuation he should have outgrown. That the way they'd lived their time together had as much to do with the clarity of his memories as the woman herself. Watching her sleep, he knew better.

For whatever reason, the contours of her face touched him like no other. The shape of her, what he saw in her eyes when she smiled, pulled at some unknown place deep inside him.

She was there, and he was going to make love with her that night—and he was going to hold on to her and see what they had come morning.

He let out a soft breath, pushed away from the door, and walked back into the kitchen, content to let her go on sleeping and dreaming until—until dinner was ready. A broad grin spread across his face. She was here!

Nikki awoke to a black velvet night and the chirping song of crickets. She knew exactly where she was, on Josh's back porch on the sultry side of Texas. The house next door was where the gardening lady and the little boy lived.

She stretched full out and relaxed back into the hammock, deciding she liked Texas. The dry Colorado air had wreaked havoc on her system after so many years in the tropical latitudes. She felt better here, more at home, more like she belonged.

Josh watched her wake slowly, enjoying the length of bare leg hanging out of the hammock. A flip-flop dangled from her toes. He eased forward in his chair, taking a shrimp out of the ice-filled bowl on the table, but never taking his eyes off her.

A soft crackling sound drew her attention away from the quiet night beyond the screen. She rolled her head sideways and found him sitting in the dark, peeling a shrimp and watching her.

"Hi." An easy smile curved his mouth.

"Hi."

"Dinner is ready." He nodded at the table.

"What are we having?"

"Shrimp, beer, and bread. All the basics."

So far so good, she thought. He didn't seem inclined to kick her right out. Neither did he seem surprised to see her.

"Were you expecting me?" she asked.

"No."

"Were you planning on coming to Colorado?"

"No." He shook his head. He wasn't going to lie to her. He'd hoped to forget her.

"Hmm." She murmured a noncommittal sound, not knowing what to make of his answer, or of the queasiness it caused in her stomach.

"Come on over, before the beer gets warm."

Outwardly calm, inwardly cautious, she slid out of the hammock and walked to the table. He'd cut his hair, shorter than she'd ever seen it. No unruly strands swept behind his ears or brushed the collar of his black polo shirt. The style gave him a harder, cleaner look, highlighting the lean angle of his cheekbones and the dark lines of his eyebrows. It made him seem more of a stranger.

Under his ever-watchful gaze, she sat down and spent an inordinate amount of time arranging her skirt. Things were different between them, subtly awkward and not-so-subtly tense. She felt the change in his quietness. When she dared to look up, she saw it in his eyes. Suddenly she understood. He'd already reached a decision about her, about them. The pain in her stomach increased.

"I don't think I can eat," she confessed, fearing the worst.

"When was your last meal?"

"I had a milk shake on the road." Oh, why had she come like this? Unannounced, filled with expectations. She'd set herself up for rejection.

He twisted the cap off a beer and set the bottle in front of her. "I've been doing some thinking about your stomach problems," he said, picking up a shrimp and peeling off the shell. He handed it to her. "I don't think there's anything wrong with you that three regular meals a day wouldn't cure. Eat." It was a command, not a request. He tore off a hunk of bread and slathered it with butter.

Nikki bit the shrimp off near the tail and chewed. He kept peeling and putting shrimp in front of her until she had a pile to match the two big pieces of buttered bread he'd added to her plate. And all the while, he kept talking to her.

"I heard you lost your job."

The shrimp caught in her throat. She choked.

"Don't be too worried about it. Somebody else will pick you up. Drink your beer."

His confidence outweighed hers by about a hundred to one. With the help of the beer, she got the shrimp down. "David didn't think so. He's . . . uh, blackballed me on the East Coast." The admission came hard, but the professional turn of the conversation was a minor relief. Bad as her employment situation was, it wasn't what kept her awake at night.

"Idle threats. You're good. Everybody knows it. Have you sent your résumé out?"

"No," she said softly, returning an untouched piece of bread to her plate. She felt awful. She couldn't eat.

"Why not?" He paused with his beer halfway to his mouth, his head tilted in curiosity.

"I don't know." She shrugged. The strap of her slip fell off her shoulder beneath the cap sleeve of her white shirt. With a distracted move, she pulled it back up. "Maybe I need a little time off."

"For what?"

*To give myself some breathing room. To find out where I stand in life besides in the middle of political upheaval. To find out about you, and me . . . and love.* She slowly looked up to meet his gaze across the table. "I don't know what to say, Josh."

Her hesitancy stripped away the years, leaving her as unsure as she'd been one summer night so long ago. She'd come because she loved him, because her days and nights felt empty without him, and she didn't know how to say those things to the man sitting across from her. Nikki Kydd, ace reporter, war correspondent, was at a loss for words.

Josh watched uncertainty cloud her eyes, seeing the telltale signs of distress come over her. He wished he could tell her everything was going to be okay, but he didn't know himself what the future held for them. They both took professional risks for granted, but he'd only risked his heart once, and he'd paid dearly for the loss. That she'd come to find him told him she'd been paying dearly too.

"Nice place you've got here," she whispered, taking refuge in the inane statement, before his silence consumed her. She forced her gaze away, looked around the porch, focused on a distant spot of moon-shadowed lawn. "How did you find it?"

"My family used to come here when I was a kid. A couple of my dad's brothers lived in Port Arthur. We'd all go fishing, have family reunions, that sort of thing. I think the fishing drove my mother nuts. One of my uncles still lives across town. My aunt Rosa lives down the street."

"You bought this house?" she asked, clued in by his tone of voice.

"A year ago. The price was right, and I needed a place to come home to. Sometimes"—he smiled slightly—"*most* of the time these last few years, when I was on assignment, the thing I hated most was the feeling of impermanence, of not having one special place that was mine."

"And before?"

His smile disappeared and a gentle longing darkened his eyes. "Before I started hating it, I had you, Nikki. You were home." His voice trailed off into a silence filled with the soft heat and night sounds of summer.

Nikki stared at her plate, unable to face the sadness she'd caused between them. Leaving had seemed right at the time. Not easy, but right. Given another chance, knowing the loneliness she'd feel, the chances she'd have to take, she'd try another way. At eighteen, she hadn't been able to see this far into the future.

"Are you finished eating?"

"Yes." The word was barely a whisper.

He rose from the table and picked up her plate. "Maybe you'll do better at breakfast."

She doubted it, doubted if she'd even be there for breakfast. She didn't want to run again, but neither did she want to continue hurting them both by trying to hang on to something she'd already thrown away.

His footsteps faded into the kitchen, and she walked over to the screen door. A warm breeze rustled the leaves on the trees, wafting the scent of flowers onto the porch. *Josh's home.* The thought crossed her mind slowly, filling her with heartache. He'd found his place, his refuge from all the chaos in the world. She was happy for him.

*So why are you crying?*

*Because he found it without me.*

She smeared the tears across her cheek and took a deep breath. This was crazy, hanging around and working herself into the blues. He had never planned on coming to Colorado, not even when she'd left him in San Simeon. Take the hint, Kydd, she told herself. Make a clean break.

"How's your mother doing?" His voice came from close behind her.

"Better than any of us expected, physically." She steadied herself with another lung-filling breath. "My Aunt Chloe is cooking up a storm, trying to fatten her up, but Mom always was slender. The hardest thing for her is adjusting to freedom and accepting Victor's death. They were only married for a year, but she did love him."

"Is she in therapy?"

"Three times a week. My mom's a big believer in taking care of problems."

"Like her daughter."

Nikki thought she'd made a pretty good mess of her problems, so she didn't say anything.

"I met her in Sulaco, before she left," he continued, moving to her side and resting his shoulder against the screen door. "We had a long talk. She's a strong lady, Nikki. I know you'll always worry about her, but she's going to come out okay."

"I think so too." Now was the moment to make her break, to find the right words, to say good-bye.

"What about you?" he asked softly, surprising her.

She made a slight turn and glanced up at him. His eyes, darkened by the night, met hers, clear and penetrating and close, so very close.

He bent his head and brushed his lips gently across hers, tasting her tears. "Why are you crying?" he murmured, his hand sliding up to cup her face.

"I . . . miss . . . you," she said between his brief, teasing kisses, feeling new tears replace the ones she'd brushed away.

"Don't miss me tonight, Nicolita." He followed the dampness up her face, kissing her cheek, her temple, her brow. "Stay for a while." His hands framed her face, lifting her mouth to his. He kissed her long and fully, taking her sadness inside himself and giving back sweet love.

His mouth moved tenderly over hers. The strength and warmth of him wrapped around her. He tightened his arms and drew her closer.

Nikki sank against him for everlasting seconds, stealing a share of the pleasure found in his kisses, in his hard body pressed to hers, in the strong arms holding her. It would be so easy to convince herself that this was all they needed, this intoxicating excitement spreading through her from the inside out. His mouth was warm, wet, consummately skilled in the erotic dance.

But she was no longer a young girl, and in all her

life, nothing had taught her more about the pain of consequences than the loving and leaving of Joshua Rios. The flash of reason shocked her into breaking off the kiss. She stepped back, saw the confusion narrowing his eyes, and she wondered when she'd grown up. A heartbeat ago, she'd held everything she wanted in her arms, or so she thought.

"I'm in over my head." Without meaning to, she spoke her thoughts aloud.

"Me too . . . but I'm willing to take a risk."

The rough sound of his voice startled her into looking back up. "Josh, we need to talk."

*A woman*, he thought with a ragged sigh, closing his eyes and leaning his head back against the door. He'd found the answer to Quico's question. Yes, Nikki was a woman now. After a moment, he opened his eyes and looked down at her. "Talking is just one of the things we need to do, Nikki, but we're not going to do it here. Come on." He slipped his hand inside hers and drew her into the kitchen, across the living room, and up the stairs to the second floor.

"Where are we going?" she asked, looking over her shoulder at the relative safety of the living room they were leaving behind.

"My bedroom. It's a great place to talk. Believe me. I've been talking to myself in there every night for the last four weeks, and mostly I was talking about you, so you should feel right at home." He mounted the stairs with purposeful strides, barely giving her a chance to protest.

"I don't think this is what I . . . what I had in mind," she stammered.

"And I think it's exactly what you had in mind. It's certainly what I had in mind, what I've had in mind for the last three years." He strode into the bedroom, released her hand, and immediately stripped off his shirt. "You might as well take your clothes off and get comfortable. We're here for the duration."

His matter-of-fact tone shocked her almost as much as his suggestion. "I will not." She enunciated every syllable with conviction. "And neither will you!" she added with alarm when his hands went to his belt buckle.

"Don't be shy, Nikki." He turned on the bedside lamp, which was in the middle of the large oak-floored room, next to the bed. The perimeter of the room was filled with a couple of desks—one holding a typewriter, the other a computer—their respective swivel chairs, a stereo system, and a pair of filing cabinets. A ream of paper spilled over the typewriter desk. A ribbon of computer paper flowed off the other. "And don't worry. I'm not going to seduce you again."

"Again?" She jerked her attention back to him, and her breath caught in her throat. Whether by accident or by design, she'd forgotten how beautiful he was, how light and shadow played across the muscles of his chest and arms, how warm and dark his skin looked. She curled her fingers into her palms and stared helplessly at him.

"Like the last time, the first time," he explained, crossing the room to her and stopping a mere breath away. He raised his hands to the top button on her blouse. She quickly covered them with her own, but his fingers stayed put. One eyebrow lifted over dark-ening blue eyes, and he pushed the first button through. "I was in bad shape that night, Nikki, more than a little desperate." Another button slipped through his fingers and hers, and the buttonhole. "When I came to your room, I thought we could just talk"—he softly emphasized the word—"but then you started to cry, and I knew I wasn't leaving without having you, whatever it took. I never gave you a chance after that, not one.

"But tonight"—he'd worked his way down to the waistband of her skirt, and he slipped his hand inside—"tonight I'm going to give you every chance you want, every chance you need." Her skirt fell to the floor. His hands slid up her body to her shoulders, burning a path across her breasts before pushing her blouse off her arms. "You can say yes . . . no . . . maybe. You can tease me, Nikki. I won't mind, but I'm not going to seduce you. You're a woman now, and women don't like being seduced. They like to . . . talk." His gaze drifted from her face to her breasts, hidden by the delicate flowering of lace on her slip. He took a deep breath and let it out. "So what do you want to talk about?"

She tried to speak, possibly to argue the definition of seduction, but the moment she opened her mouth, he rubbed his hands over her shoulders, taking her slip straps with them.

"Hmm?" he questioned, his thick lashes shadowing the languid light in his eyes.

He'd mesmerized her with touch, she thought, proving the truth of his words. She had come to love him, and he was making it so very easy. The remembered magic of that long-ago night, of the year they'd spent together sharing their friendship and their lives, had never left her. She wanted to belong somewhere, too, to belong to him.

"Okay, Nikki." He sighed. "I'll start . . . here." His right hand slid up her bare thigh, pushing her slip higher and higher, and sending shimmers of lightning-quick pleasure across her skin. "And here," he murmured, his mouth opening over her ear. He rested his arm on her shoulder, leaning across her and bracing his left hand on the wall. Then he began, teasing her with whispers and the overwhelming, gentle pressures of his body. "You've stopped crying. I'm glad. I don't want you to cry anymore." His tongue traced the inside of her ear, and a path of heat raced down the side of her neck. "Let me love you, Nicolita, before you drive me crazy. Let go of your fear and . . . let go of your slip."

He reinforced his husky command with tugs on the soft material. The friction of silk sliding down her breasts gave way to hot masculine skin rubbing against hers. His low groan of pleasure vibrated through her body, lowering the last barriers of resistance.

She felt foolish and easy, and as if she were dying inside. The undeniable swelling between his legs, the hard muscles in his arms, the wet, gentle gnawing of his mouth on her neck, along her jaw, under her chin, laid waste to her thoughts before they could form, leaving her with nothing to hold on to except the slick strength of his body. She was lost, completely lost to the one undeniable truth she'd kept sacred.

"Oh, yes, Josh. I missed you. Every day and every—"

His mouth slid over hers, stealing her words with tenderness. She turned her head, and his tongue slipped between her lips, its lazy, sweeping track a sweet counterpoint to the urgency of his arousal pressing against the soft swell of her tummy. Holding her with just the passion of his kiss, his mouth consuming hers with deep strokes, he moved his hands between their bodies and worked his zipper down. Then he replaced his hands with both of hers, guiding her in pushing his pants and underwear off his hips and down his thighs, where they slid from her grasp to the floor.

"And every night," he murmured, "I thought of you and how you had loved me."

His breath whispered across her lips, then stopped as her hands journeyed over him. When she lingered too long, he showed her what he wanted, where he needed her touch. A ragged sigh tore from his throat as she closed her hand around him.

"Sometimes," he said hoarsely, "I hated you for running away, and sometimes I hurt until I thought I'd lose my mind." A surprising, soft smile curved his lips and warmed his eyes to smoky blue. "Which could happen at any moment. Come on, Nikki," he growled. "Wrap your legs around me. Pour the life back into me." Kicking out of his pants and leaving her slip in a creamy white pile on the floor, he slid his hands under her bottom and lifted her into his arms.

Nikki clung to him, drawn by his strength and her own pulsing need for immediate sensual survival. The pleasure coursing through her knew no limits and only one irresistible destination. She covered his face with hot kisses, trailing her tongue across his cheek for a taste of her lover, letting her hair fall over his shoulders and encase them in a golden veil. They needed a safe, secret place for their shared rediscovery of what love had been, what it would be again, a place that went no further than their skin and yet opened to an endless universe inside.

Her fingers tunneled through his hair as her mouth opened over his, drawing his breath into her. At his first step, she linked her ankles at the small of his back and sank into the small rocking explosions of his body against hers.

Josh tightened his arms around her. He'd won her back, and all he'd had to do was run a gauntlet of danger, desperation, and lethal weapons. All he'd had to do was slam his back against a wall and put his life on the line. And he'd had to wait, but the waiting was over. She'd never been an easy woman to hold on to at any age, but he'd won her back for tonight, for a second chance. He wanted to shout his victory, wanted to laugh aloud in triumph, but the wild sweetness of Nikki in love turned his shouts into hungry groans, turned his victory and his triumph into raw desire.

He lowered her to the bed and pressed her deep into the mattress with his weight, his mouth plundering the hidden delights of hers and capturing her soft moans of pleasure. The languorous glide of her foot down his thigh and calf fascinated him with memories of the release to come, but he didn't want to take her yet, not until he'd tasted and savored every creamy, satiny inch of her.

He started with a tantalizing journey to her breasts, turning his head from side to side to take them both in from rise to peak. He wanted to consume her as the heat she generated consumed him, completely but slowly, leaving mere heartbeats between the sizzling bolts of ecstasy.

Nikki was on the verge of a precipice, needing only one special touch of his mouth to make her fall. But he teased her, played with her, and drew her pleasure almost to pain before he took the peak of her breast into his mouth. Her softly murmured sighs urged him on. The melting of her body beneath his intoxicated him. She was open so fully, her legs already around him, her arms stretching above her head in a feline response to the erotic strokes of his tongue.

"Ah, Nikki . . ." He slowed the teasing caress, his muscles straining with the effort not to take her.

"Help me, Josh," she whispered, her eyes drifting open, revealing the pale green fire within. "Help me." She lifted her hips and pushed at the white lace panties still between them.

The delicate force of her body torched his arousal to a fever pitch, and with one sure move, he slipped the scrap of lingerie off her legs. Then, with aching slowness, he slid his fingers back up the same silky length, molding the slender curves of her thighs and going farther to the alluring mystery nestled in between.

His gaze followed his dark hand against her creamy skin until he began to slide within, pleasuring her and easing the way for greater pleasure. At that moment, he lifted his gaze to hers and bathed himself in the sultry fire in her eyes. Her quivering response to his touch, and the unconscious track of her tongue across her lips made waiting any longer an impossibility.

He leaned over her and with his tongue followed the wet trail she'd left on her mouth. He kissed her gently, sweetly, lingering until he knew she was ready.

"You are beautiful, *querida mía*," he murmured, his voice rough with emotion. "More beauty than I've ever known. *Tanto que te quiero.* I love you so much . . . so much . . . "

He entered her then, sliding into her satin heat and watching enchantment steal her breath even as it stole his own. She held him deeper with each rhythmic surge, until his name was a cry on her lips and her body was molten gold in his arms. His kisses became wilder as they neared the peak, his breathing labored, his thrusts stronger, his love boundless. The gift he demanded, the gift she gave, was everything of herself. The gift she accepted in return was everything he had to offer. She took the exquisite pleasure he gave with his body. She took the boundless love he gave with his heart.

And when he surged into her for the last time, they poured their lives into each other.

Nikki held him, knowing she'd found her home and her love in his arms, in his smile, in the words he whispered so sweetly. She knew she'd never leave him, and she hoped and prayed that this time he would ask her to stay.

# *Fourteen*

"I think you've put on some weight."

"Tell me something I don't know," Nikki drawled, walking onto the back porch with the day's mail in her hands. "I've been eating nonstop for a week."

"How's your tummy?"

"My tummy is fine." She slanted him a look over the top of one of the letters, an impish grin on her face. She tapped the envelope on her nose. "Another apology from David. I really should call him, put him out of his misery."

"Let him sweat it out awhile longer. Firing Nikki Kydd," Josh scoffed. "The man's got more nerve than brains." He reached for her as she passed the hammock.

Nikki felt his arm encircle her waist, and in the next moment she was tumbled backward into the hammock. "Josh!"

"Nikki!" He feigned amazement, trapping her with his leg thrown over hers. A wolfish gleam lit his eyes, and he wrapped his arms around her, capturing her completely. "You have put on weight. I can't feel your ribs."

"Don't!" she gasped, stifling a giggle under the ticklish foray of his fingers.

He desisted, pressing a light kiss to her forehead. "What do you want to do today?" He settled back into the hammock and pushed the floor with his foot, setting them to swinging.

Nikki snuggled up to him, feeling herself fill with the love they'd found, but her words were serious. "I think one of us should find a job, before we sink so far into poverty we're living on beans and rice."

"I've got a job," he said, his hand absently trailing up her arm. He smiled at the concern in her voice and thought back to the notebook she'd carried and worried over their first year together. She'd written every day's expenditures in that book, trying to balance them with an unreliable flow of earnings, trying to keep them solvent. Some things would never change, he mused. Like his love for her.

"Hah!" she exclaimed, rolling over to face him. "That rag you work for isn't going to keep paying you indefinitely. Sooner rather than later they're going to want to see some results from this little sabbatical you've declared for yourself."

He looked up at the sweet angel face over his, at the silky silver-gold ponytail tracing the delicate curve of her cheeks and hanging across her shoulder, and he knew he had everything he wanted. "You worry too much. Besides, I'm not on sabbatical. I'm on vacation."

"Forever?"

"No, just until the weekend. Panama is heating up again. They want me to go back down and cover the elections."

Suddenly Nikki wished she hadn't brought the subject up. They'd been living in a dream world these last few days, a world made up of the two of them, the house, and the Gulf of Mexico under sunny skies. She'd known it couldn't go on forever, and she'd wanted something solid to hold on to in the future. But Panama! Panama was no future at all.

"Don't go," she blurted, and was instantly embarrassed by the ridiculous outburst. She sank down into the hammock, the tips of her fingers touching her mouth.

"Maybe I won't," he said softly, staring at the ceiling.

"What?" She pushed herself back up and looked at him, surprised.

"Maybe I won't go," he repeated, his gaze shifting to meet hers.

"Why not?"

He tried not to smile. She sounded wary, unsure, a little off balance—just the way he wanted her. He shrugged, negating the importance of her question.

"Well," she said, "maybe I should give your editor a call. If they need someone down there and they're willing to pay . . ."

"I don't think so," he drawled. "I did some checking. The Panamanians won't let you in the country. Something about actions unbefitting a journalist, a belief held by more than half of Latin America. You're persona non grata just about everyplace south of the Rio Grande, Nikki. Nobody wants you within striking distance of their government."

"Me!" she gasped, her professional ire rising to flaming heights. "What about you? You're the one who skulduggered around and tore Travinas to bits!"

"Skulduggered?" He cocked an eyebrow.

"You know what I mean."

"Yes, I do. But as far as they know, I did everything according to standard journalistic practices and—"

"Standard journalistic practices!" she interrupted, shock showing in her eyes. "Passing yourself off as Juan Alonso and infiltrating—"

He lifted his head and silenced her with a quick kiss. "Shh, Nikki. It doesn't matter. You've got the rest of the world to choose from."

She let his words sink in, felt them mollify the worst of her anger and take the edge off her wounded pride. She ignored the other realms of her emotions, the parts that had waited patiently and in vain for him to ask her to stay. She'd taken each day's love as it came and slowly accepted a hard truth: Kydd and Rios were a byline, stolen moments of time for sharing love and friendship, but not the stuff of her latent dreams.

"Great," she said, hiding the hurt with sarcasm. "What am I supposed to do with the rest of the world? Central America is my beat. Maybe I should get on the phone to David and tell him I'm ready to come back to work."

"I had something else in mind." He was losing her again, and he wasn't going to allow that to happen. "Something that should appeal to your predilection for living on the edge."

"I'm not going to the Middle East," she said flatly, crossing her arms over her chest. Then, almost reluctantly, she added, "I didn't want to go back to Central America either. The edge has . . . lost its charm."

"What do you want, Nikki?"

"The middle ground." She half lifted her hand in a gesture toward the neighboring house. It was a new kind of risk, exposing her weakness for him to see. He'd fallen in love with a wild young girl, someone who'd met danger at his side, someone who'd gone to any length for a story and her mother's freedom.

But she'd changed, been tempered by the passing years and the acceptance of her own mortality. She had her mother. Now she wanted other things.

Josh followed the direction of her gesture to the quiet house next door, then looked back at her. "Not much action over there. Not much fame. Damn little glory. Are you sure, Nikki?"

"I'm sure of what I want." She hesitated and looked at him. "But I'm not sure how, or if, I can get it."

Josh lay very quiet, watching the steady rhythm of her pulse and the lifting and falling of shadows across her face. The hammock slowed in its swaying, and still he watched her.

She forced a fleeting smile to her lips. "Crazy, huh?"

He nodded in agreement, his face solemn, his eyes dark and searching. Then he leaned close and whispered in her ear. "I love you."

"I know, but—"

"No reservations, Nikki. I love you." He kissed her cheek and settled back into the hammock. It was time to pop the proverbial question. *The* proverbial question. "I've been doing a little thinking."

Chicken, he thought, giving his head a shake. He'd have to do better than that.

Something in his manner told Nikki he'd been doing a lot of thinking. She gave him a quizzical glance. "Thinking about what?"

Josh did an internal check of his pulse and decided to slide into the question. "You."

"Me?"

"And me." He wondered how long he could drag the moment out, and whether or not it would help or hinder his cause. Despite her recent track record, and her most recent confession, he knew Nikki had the heart of a free-lancer. She was used to being on her own, in charge of her own life, coming and going as she pleased.

"What about you . . . and me?" she asked, becoming strangely still beside him.

"I was thinking of a new partnership." There, he'd said it. He felt a tremendous weight lift from his chest.

Which came crashing back down with her softly spoken "Oh."

He suddenly wished they'd spent more time talking and less time making love the past week. Their communications obviously needed some work. On the other hand, he wouldn't have missed a minute he'd spent with her in his bed, their bed.

" 'Oh' isn't an option in this instance, Nikki," he said, keeping his gaze glued to the ceiling. "When a man asks you to marry him, you have the choice of saying yes or no, not 'oh.' "

He felt her sharp intake of breath. He hazarded a quick glance and found her staring at him through wide, surprised eyes.

"Marriage? You and me?" she said, her voice high and incredulous.

"I think we can handle it."

"Oh, Josh, are you sure? You know how we fight, and heaven knows I'll never forgive myself for dragging you into that mess in—"

He rolled over on top of her, his mouth covering hers in a passionate kiss, stealing her breath and her words. He released her and gave her a warning glance. "Don't try to talk me out of this, Nicolita, not while I'm trying so hard to talk you into it. You probably saved my life in San Simeon. If it hadn't been for you, Brazia would have cornered me in Panama. Coming after you is the only reason I wasn't where he thought I'd be."

"Josh, I still—"

He kissed her again, slowly and deeply, pressing his body against her in the preamble to love. "I love you," he said huskily. "I want you for my wife. I'll give you all the small-town living you can take, and when you get bored, I'll let you get us both in trouble until we have to come running back. Say yes, Nikki. That's all I ask, a simple yes, meaning forever."

"Yes." She sighed and pulled him back down. Her mouth played across his, promising him the lifetime he asked. After she'd kissed him, and kissed him again, she angled her mouth away from his. "I've got an idea."

"Me too. Lots of them," he said and groaned softly as she shifted beneath him.

"A great idea," she insisted, meeting his eyes with a smile of pure mischief.

"It couldn't be any better than mine. Would you do that again?"

"What?"

"Move like . . . yeah, just like that." He groaned again and gently rocked against her, his mouth settling into the curve of her neck. "Ah, Nikki, what you do to me."

"Rios and Rios," she said breathlessly, melting under the sweet pressure he applied. "No one knows Nicolita Rios. We could go down and cover . . . Panama."

"I thought you didn't want to go back down south," he murmured against her skin, his hand sliding under her shirt.

"I'll go anywhere with you." Words became more difficult to find with each tender caress of his fingers across her breasts.

"How about upstairs?"

"Anywhere."

"Good. Now forget about Panama and all the trouble you've got in store for me"—eyes warmed by a sultry light lifted to meet hers—"and think about loving me the way I love you, Nicolita. Way down deep inside, every day and every night, through all the bad times and good times to come."

"This is one of the good times, Josh," she said softly, feeling the security of his love wrap around her future and make it bright.

"Yes, Nikki," he agreed with a sly smile teasing his mouth. "This is one of the really, really good times."

Later, in the fading light of day, as they lay facing each other on the bed in the middle of the room, Nikki gently traced his scar with her finger.

"Why did you let me think all those wild things about you that first year?"

"Because you were young and impressionable, and I was trying like hell to impress you." He caught her hand and pressed a kiss into her palm.

"Why?"

He laughed. "Because you were too cocky and too pretty to ignore, and too young to take to bed."

"And a year made all the difference?"

"You were still too young to take to bed"—he shook his head ruefully—"but by then you were impossible to ignore. Three more years didn't change that. A hundred years won't change it. You're mine, Nikki. I stopped questioning why a long time ago."

Sliding her hand around his neck, she drew him close into her arms. "So did I, Josh," she whispered. "So did I."

# THE EDITOR'S CORNER

We suspect that Cupid comes to visit our Bantam offices every year when we're preparing the Valentine's Day books. It seems we're always specially inspired by the one exclusively romantic holiday in the year. And our covers next month reflect just how inspired we were . . . by our authors who also must have had a visit from the chubby cherub. They shimmer with cherry-red metallic ink and are presents in and of themselves—as are the stories within. They range from naughty to very nice!

First, we bring you Suzanne Forster's marvelous **WILD CHILD**, LOVESWEPT #384. Cat D'Angelo had been the town's bad girl and Blake Wheeler its golden boy when the young assistant D.A. had sent her to the reformatory for suspected car theft. Now, ten years later, she has returned to work as a counselor to troubled kids—and to even the score with the man who had hurt her so deeply! Time had only strengthened the powerful forces that drew them together . . . and Blake felt inescapable hunger for the beautiful, complicated hellcat who could drive a man to ruin—or to ecstasy. Could the love and hate Cat had held so long in her heart be fused by the fire of mutual need and finally healed by passion? We think you'll find **WILD CHILD** delicious—yet calorie free—as chocolates packaged in a red satin box!

Treat yourself to a big bouquet with Gail Douglas's *The Dreamweavers:* **BEWITCHING LADY**, LOVESWEPT #385. When the Brawny Josh Campbell who looked as if he could wield a sword as powerfully as any clansman stopped on a deserted road to give her a ride, Heather Sinclair played a mischievous Scottish lass to the hilt, beguiling the moody but fascinating man whose gaze hid inner demons . . . and hinted at a dangerous passion she'd never known. Josh felt his depression lift after months of despair, but he was too cynical to succumb to this delectable minx's appeal . . . or was he? A true delight!

Sweet, fresh-baked goodies galore are yours in Joan
*(continued)*

Elliott Pickart's **MIXED SIGNALS,** LOVESWEPT #386. Katha Logan threw herself into Vince Santini's arms, determined to rescue the rugged ex-cop from the throng of reporters outside city hall. Vince enjoyed being kidnapped by this lovely and enchanting nut who drove like a madwoman and intrigued him with her story of a crime he just *had* to investigate . . . with her as his partner! Vince believed that a man who risked his life for a living had no business falling in love. Katha knew she could cherish Vince forever if he'd let her, but playing lovers' games wasn't enough anymore. Could they learn to fly with the angels and together let their passions soar?

We give a warm, warm greeting—covered with hearts, with flowers—to a new LOVESWEPT author, but one who's not new to any of us who treasure romances. Welcome Lori Copeland, who brings us LOVESWEPT #387, **DARLING DECEIVER,** next month. Bestselling mystery writer Shae Malone returned to the sleepy town where he'd spent much of his childhood to finish his new novel, but instead of peace and quiet, he found his home invaded by a menagerie of zoo animals temporarily living next door . . . with gorgeously grown-up Harriet Whitlock! As a teenager she'd chased him relentlessly, embarrassed him with poems declaring everlasting love, but now she was an exquisite woman whose long-legged body made him burn with white-hot fire. Harri still wanted Shae with shameless abandon, but did she dare risk giving her heart again?

Your temperature may rise when you read **HEARTTHROB** by Doris Parmett, LOVESWEPT #388. Hannah Morgan was bright, eager, beautiful—an enigma who filled television director Zack Matthews with impatience . . . and a sizzling hunger. The reporter in him wanted to uncover her mysteries, while the man simply wanted to gaze at her in moonlight. Hannah was prepared to work as hard as she needed to satisfy the workaholic heartbreaker . . . until her impossibly virile boss crumbled her defenses with tenderness and ignited a hunger she'd never expected to feel again. Was she
*(continued)*

willing to fight to keep her man? Don't miss this sparkling jewel of a love story. A true Valentine's Day present.

For a great finish to a special month, don't miss Judy Gill's **STARGAZER**, LOVESWEPT #389, a romance that shines with the message of the power of love . . . at any age. As the helicopter hovered above her, Kathy M'Gonigle gazed with wonder at her heroic rescuer, but stormy-eyed Gabe Fowler was furious at how close she'd come to drowning in the sudden flood—and shocked at the joy he felt at touching her again! Years before, he'd made her burn with desire, but she'd been too young and he too restless to settle down. Now destiny had brought them both home. Could the man who put the stars in her eyes conquer the past and promise her forever?

All our books—well, their authors wish they could promise you forever. That's not possible, but authors and staff can wish you wonderful romance reading.

Now it is my great pleasure to give you one more Valentine's gift—namely, to reintroduce you to our Susann Brailey, now Senior Editor, who will grace these pages in the future with her fresh and enthusiastic words. But don't think for a minute that you're getting rid of me! I'll be here—along with the rest of the staff—doing the very best to bring you wonderful love stories all year long.

As I have told you many times in the past, I wish you peace, joy, and the best of all things—the love of family and friends.

*Carolyn Nichols*

Carolyn Nichols
Editor
*LOVESWEPT*
Bantam Books
666 Fifth Avenue
New York, NY 10103

## FAN OF THE MONTH

### Joni Clayton

It's really great fun to be a LOVESWEPT Fan of the Month as it provides me with the opportunity to publicly thank Carolyn Nichols, Bantam Books, and some of my favorite authors: Sandra Brown, Iris Johansen, Kay Hooper, Fayrene Preston, Helen Mittermeyer and Deborah Smith (to name only a few!).

My good friend, Mary, first introduced me to romance fiction and LOVESWEPTS in 1984 as an escape from the pressures of my job. Almost immediately my associates noticed the difference in my disposition and attitude and questioned the reason for the change. They all wanted to thank LOVESWEPT!

It did not take me long to discover that most romance series were inconsistent in quality and were not always to my liking—but not LOVESWEPT. I have thoroughly enjoyed each and every volume. All were "keepers" . . . so of course I wanted to own the entire series. I enlisted the aid of friends and used book dealers. Presto! The series was complete! As soon as LOVESWEPT was offered through the mail, I subscribed and have never missed a copy!

I have since retired from the "hurly-burly" of the working world and finally have the time to start to reread all of my LOVESWEPT "keepers."

To Carolyn, all of the authors, and the LOVESWEPT staff—Thanks for making my retirement so enjoyable!

# 60 Minutes to a Better, More Beautiful You!

**N**ow it's easier than ever to awaken your sensuality, stay slim forever—even make yourself irresistible. With Bantam's bestselling subliminal audio tapes, you're only 60 minutes away from a better, more beautiful you!

| | | |
|---|---|---|
| __ 45004-2 | **Slim Forever** | $8.95 |
| __ 45112-X | **Awaken Your Sensuality** | $7.95 |
| __ 45081-6 | **You're Irresistible** | $7.95 |
| __ 45035-2 | **Stop Smoking Forever** | $8.95 |
| __ 45130-8 | **Develop Your Intuition** | $7.95 |
| __ 45022-0 | **Positively Change Your Life** | $8.95 |
| __ 45154-5 | **Get What You Want** | $7.95 |
| __ 45041-7 | **Stress Free Forever** | $7.95 |
| __ 45106-5 | **Get a Good Night's Sleep** | $7.95 |
| __ 45094-8 | **Improve Your Concentration** | $7.95 |
| __ 45172-3 | **Develop A Perfect Memory** | $8.95 |

**Bantam Books, Dept. LT, 414 East Golf Road, Des Plaines, IL 60016**

Please send me the items I have checked above. I am enclosing $_____ (please add $2.00 to cover postage and handling). Send check or money order, no cash or C.O.D.s please. (Tape offer good in USA only.)

Mr/Ms _____

Address _____

City/State _____ Zip _____

LT-12/89

Please allow four to six weeks for delivery.
Prices and availability subject to change without notice.

# THE DELANEY DYNASTY

Men and women whose loves an passions are so glorious it takes many great romance novels by three bestselling authors to tell their tempestuous stories.

## THE SHAMROCK TRINITY

## THE DELANEYS OF KILLAROO

## THE DELANEYS: *The Untamed Years*